Praise for Dear Dylan

'Tender, quirky and cool. Siobhan Curham is a name to watch' *Cathy Cassidy*

'An absorbing, moving novel . . . I'm still thinking about the characters so much that I want check on them and see how things are going for them now!' *Luisa Plaja, Chicklish*

'A funny, moving, thought-provoking story about a very special friendship' *Tabitha Suzuma*

'Reminds us of the power of true friendships. A wonderful achievement' *Booktrust*

'A great, fast-paced read. All I can say is, "GO, GEORGIE!"' *Bookalicious Ramblings*

'I didn't want to leave these characters behind. A wonderful read full of laughs, tears and heart' *Carrie's YA Bookshelf*

'Truly a diamond of a novel. Touching, funny and full of heart; I just couldn't get enough' *Lauren's Crammed Bookshelf*

'A story to lighten the soul. I laughed and cried and wanted more' *Tales of a Ravenous Reader*

'Fabulous . . . poignant . . . honest' *The Sweet Bonjour*

'Touching and emotional . . . really special' *So Many Books, So Little Time*

'Strong and realistic characters that people of all ages will relate to' *A Life Bound By Books*

'Keeps the reader captivated from start to finish. Intimate and honest . . . I loved it' *I Was a Teenage Book Geek*

'A very beautiful story. You're going to love it' *Darlyn & Books*

'I really couldn't put it down' *Sarah's Book Reviews*

'A fab story' *The Overflowing Lib*

SIOBHAN CURHAM

Hi there!

Whenever I sit down to read a book I always have two questions lurking in the back of my mind. Number one, why did the author choose to write this particular story and number two, where did they write it? So if you're like me and have these same two questions about *Dear Dylan*, let me tell you the answers. Number one, I wanted to write about the importance of never giving up on your dreams. And number two, I wrote it in a cupboard.

In *Dear Dylan* the main character, Georgie, dreams of being an actress, but problems at home are making her life extremely difficult. By showing how Georgie faces these problems I wanted to inspire readers to chase their own dreams, no matter how tough life gets.

And as for the cupboard – I read somewhere that every writer should have a room of their own in which they can write, uninterrupted. As I wasn't lucky enough to have a spare room I managed to squash a tiny desk and laptop into my bedroom cupboard and spent six months writing amongst a rail of clothes. It certainly was an interesting experience!

For more information about my writing please visit www.electricmonkeybooks.co.uk or find me on Facebook.

I do hope you enjoy *Dear Dylan* and remember – never, ever give up on your dreams!

Dear Dylan...

SIOBHAN CURHAM

Dear Dylan
First published 2010 by Authorhouse
Published 2012 by Electric Monkey, an imprint of Egmont UK Limited
239 Kensington High Street, London W8 6SA

Text copyright © 2010 Siobhan Curham
The moral rights of the author have been asserted

ISBN 978 1 4052 6037 4

1 3 5 7 9 10 8 6 4 2

www.electricmonkeybooks.co.uk

A CIP catalogue record for this title is available from the British Library

50041/1

Typeset by Avon DataSet Ltd, Bidford on Avon, Warwickshire
Printed and bound in Great Britain by CPI Group

MIX
Paper
FSC FSC® C018306

EGMONT

Our story began over a century ago, when seventeen-year-old Egmont Harald Petersen found a coin in the street. He was on his way to buy a flyswatter, a small hand-operated printing machine that he then set up in his tiny apartment.

The coin brought him such good luck that today Egmont has offices in over 30 countries around the world. And that lucky coin is still kept at the company's head offices in Denmark.

For my parents, Anne and Mikey

— thank you.

Contents

Part One

E-Mates

From: georgie*harris@hotmail.com
To: info@dylancurtland.com
Date: Mon, 22 May 16:05
Subject: Love

Dear Dylan,

Oh my God, this feels really weird, writing you an email as if I know you or something! But the thing is, I really feel as if I do know you. And – here goes – I love you. I know we haven't met or anything, but sometimes when I watch you in Jessop Close I feel as if you're talking just to me. I mean, I know you're not really talking just to me. I know there are 7.6 million other viewers you're talking to too. If I thought you were talking just to me, well, I'd be a bit of a weirdo mentalist (as my best friend Jessica R. Bailey would say) and I'm not a weirdo mentalist, honest. It's just that sometimes when you're arguing with your parents, or when you confide in Mark or Kez, the things you say, well, it's as if you're speaking my own private thoughts. Does that make sense? Probably not. But what I'm trying to say is that I understand. I know what it's like to be an outsider. And it's only when I watch you in Jessop Close and you say the things you do that I don't feel so completely alone.

11

Because at least I know that someone else out there feels the same way as me. I know you're an actor, and my absolute fave actor by the way. The other girls at school all love Jeremy Bridges but I'm sorry, he's just a snoron if you ask me. I think you ought to know that I like to make up new words. A snoron is a moron who is so boring he makes you want to snore. You are way more interesting than Jeremy Bridges and at least you aren't going out with a supermodel who thinks it's smart to get out of cars wearing no knickers when she knows there are going to be loads of photographers around. Just out of interest, are you going out with anyone right now? But anyway, as I was saying, I know you're an actor and the things you say are all part of a script, but it's the way you say them. You couldn't be that convincing if you didn't really understand what it felt like. Could you?

I hope I didn't shock you when I said that I loved you. It's just that I was watching Oprah this morning and she said that we should all tell each other we love each other a whole lot more. She said the world would be a much better place and there wouldn't be wars and terrorism and stuff if we did. We're not supposed to tell everyone of course, there is NO WAY I would tell my scummy stepdad that I loved him because that would be lying and I don't think Oprah would want that. I made a list of everyone I love on the back of my mum's shopping list. It goes like this:

Dylan Curtland aka you!
Michaela Roberts
Angelica Roberts
Jessica R. Bailey
Jeff Harris

Jessica R. Bailey has been my best friend since we met in junior school — we're now in Year 9. The 'R' stands for Rebecca, and Jessica thinks it sounds dead sophisticated when people use their middle initials. My middle name is Olivia, so that makes me Georgie O. Harris, which makes me sound more like an Irish builder than a sophisticated person, but there you go. Michaela Roberts is my four-year-old sister and Angelica Roberts is my mum. She doesn't like me calling her Angelica because she says it sounds like I'm not her daughter, but I usually call her it in my head. I love the way it sounds like a cross between 'angel' and 'delicate'. It's the perfect name for her. My dad (Jeff Harris) used to call her Angel, because that's what she looks like, with snowy white skin and little rosebud cheeks and lips. But she's really delicate too. And that's the only thing I don't love about her, the feeling that one day she might break into a million tiny pieces. You might have noticed that I said my dad 'used' to call her Angel. That's because my dad is . . . well, he's dead. But I still love him. I wish I had an email address for him like I do for you. That would be so cool, wouldn't it? If heaven, or wherever we go when we die, had a website and everyone was given Hotmail accounts with instant messenger as soon as they got there. Then at least you could still talk to them after they'd gone. And they could give you advice and stuff and tell you not to worry and that everything was going to be chips. (That's what my dad used to say when he meant everything was going to be great because chips were his favourite thing in the whole world – apart from me and mum of course.)

I'm OK though, because I've still got Oprah and she gives some really frost-free advice. (Frost-free is my latest new word by the way. It means something really cool that comes with no crap, i.e. frost.) Anyway, Oprah is totally frost-free and so are you. I hope this email doesn't embarrass you. I just wanted to let you know:
I LOVE U!!!

And thank you for being so brilliant on Jessop Close. It's the only soap worth watching and that's all thanks to you.

Lots of love,
Georgie Harris – aged 14 (Juliet from 'Romeo and Juliet' was only 13, you know.)

From: info@dylancurtland.com
To: georgie*harris@hotmail.com
Date: Mon, 22 May 22:10
Subject: Re: Love

Hi there,

Many thanks for your email. I'm so glad you like my website. Please check out the 'LATEST' section for all of my latest news. Hope you have a great summer and thanks for your support.

Dylan x

....

From: georgie*harris@hotmail.com
To: info@dylancurtland.com
Date: Wed, 24 May 16:07
Subject: Thank you!!

Dear Dylan,

OMG! I can't believe I've got an email from you – and you replied so quickly as well. I thought you would have been really busy learning lines or rehearsing or filming or something. Thank you sooooo much for getting back to me straight away and I'm sorry for taking two days to get back to you, but I don't have a computer of my own at home. I only get to go online when I go to the library, and my mum wouldn't let me go to the library after school yesterday because I had to look after my kid sister Michaela. (My mum used to be a big George Michael fan by the way – even the fact that she had two girls didn't put her off naming us after him!)

I was interested that you said you were glad I liked your website. I just checked my sent mail and I didn't actually say anything about your website. Although of course I do love it and think it is totally frost-free! Especially the picture of you sitting on that gate looking out to sea, you look so thoughtful. Never mind, I guess you get loads of emails so it must be easy to get them muddled up. I was the one who said I loved you, in case you've forgotten. It's a bit embarrassing thinking about that now. I hope you don't think I'm a weirdo mentalist?!! It's just that the day I sent it I was trying really hard to turn over a new leaf. My stepdad Tone (most people think his name's short for Tony but I think it's short for tone deaf – the way he sings he makes a drill sound musical!) had said that I was a spiteful brat because I'd made Michaela cry. (Michaela is my half kid sister. She isn't half a kid, she's four now so she is a full kid, believe me, but we don't have the same dad so she's only half my sister.) Anyway I didn't make her cry on purpose. I just wanted my scissors back. I'd never be spiteful to Michaela, she's way too cute, but I suppose I could be a bit more loving, especially when I get a black cloud on (as my dad used to say). So when Oprah said . . . well anyway, I'm the person who told you she loved you and your acting and, even though I didn't write it, I love your website too. I've signed up to your mailing list and I will definitely check out your LATEST section for all your latest news.

Can't wait to see you in Jessop Close tonight – as long as Tone-Deaf lets me watch it. I've got a horrible feeling there's a football match on the other side. Thanks again for the email. I still can't believe you replied to me. That the same fingers that tried to strangle Bridget Randall in Monday night's episode – she so deserved it, the lying cow – actually typed an email to me! I will NEVER empty my inbox again!

Lots of love,
Georgie xxx

....

From: georgie*harris@hotmail.com
To: info@dylancurtland.com
Date: Wed, 7 June 15:50
Subject: URGENT!!!

Dear Dylan,

I know you must be really busy but please, PLEASE can you tell me that the rumours aren't true. Please tell me you aren't leaving Jessop Close. I don't know what I'd do if that happened.

Lots of love,
Georgie xxx

....

From: info@dylancurtland.com
To: georgie*harris@hotmail.com
Date: Thur, 15 June 10:22
Subject: Leaving Jessop Close

Hi there,

As you may have read in the press, I have decided to leave Jessop Close. Having spent five extremely enjoyable years

18

there, I feel the time is right for me to move on. After recent storylines I feel there is nowhere left to take the character of Jimmy, and I now look forward to exploring other characters both on stage and screen. I am hugely grateful to the production team at Jessop Close for the opportunity they have given me; I couldn't have wished for a better start to my acting career. Thank you so much to you too for your support, and please continue to visit my website to find out details of my new acting projects.

Dylan x

....

From: georgie*harris@hotmail.com
To: info@dylancurtland.com
Date: Thur, 15 June 16:55
Subject: Re: Leaving Jessop Close

Dear Dylan,

Oh no!!! I can't believe you're leaving the Close. This is going to sound really corny — especially after my previous confessions of love — but I actually cried when I found out! I'm crying now too, which is slightly embarrassing as I'm using a computer in the library and this gross man with yellow teeth and a greasy anorak sitting at the PC next to me keeps staring and muttering something under his breath that sounds like, 'Gimmee crumpets, gimmee crumpets'!

I actually knew the terrible news before I got your email – thanks so much for your email by the way – because I saw the story in Tone-Deaf's paper last night, and as soon as I saw the headline 'CURTAINS FOR CURTLAND!' I knew something bad had happened. Are they really going to kill you off? Can't you get them to just put you in a coma or something? Then at least you could come back. Maybe they could get you to bang your head on one of the machines in the slaughterhouse? Or have a motorbike accident on the corner of the Close – it looks like a really busy junction – and just be in hospital for a while? I know you aren't really dying, but the thing is, you will be to me because I only get to see you in Jessop Close. Once you leave there you'll be gone from my life forever.

Tone-Deaf really took the piss when he saw me crying last night. Sorry – I know you said in that interview in Bliss that you don't like girls who swear, but Tone-Deaf could make a nun swear, trust me! He said I was a baby and Michaela was more grown up than me. Hmm, Michaela, the one who thinks that tooth fairies live up electricity pylons and babies are delivered by storks. Actually, I wish I still believed that last one – anything would be better than thinking of my mum doing it with him! He just doesn't understand what it's like to be heartbroken. He doesn't understand anything unless it's got odds attached to it. If he's not out driving his cab he's in his second home – the bookies. Well, the odds of me being happy now have been slashed to 1,000,000 – 1. (That means it's so unlikely, there's more chance of the crumpet-muttering creep next to me having a shower!) The worst thing is I'm not even going to be able to watch you tonight because my mum isn't feeling too good, and when my mum gets sick I have to stay in my bedroom. Actually I don't have to stay there but it's a lot easier if I do. Oh well, I'm sure you don't want to hear about that. At least I have your email – another one to save forever in my inbox. And don't worry, I will be checking out the LATEST section on your website every day for details of your new work. Good luck Dylan, and if you ever get the time please do email me again.

Loads of love and support,
Georgie xxx

From: georgie*harris@hotmail.com
To: info@dylancurtland.com
Date: Thur, 6 July 16:07
Subject: OMG!!

Dear Dylan,

I cannot believe they electrocuted you!! I mean, of all the ways they could have killed you why did they have to choose that? And on a toaster!! For a start your character NEVER has toast for breakfast — you always grab an apple from the fruit bowl before heading off to the slaughterhouse, don't you? And secondly, would anyone really make toast while holding an open carton of juice over the toaster and standing on a wet floor? I mean, hello? The continuity people on Jessop Close really need to get their act together. I got a book called Television Drama for Dummies out of the library the other day, and I now know all about continuity and the importance of it. I've decided that one day I'd like to be an actor too — as soon as I escape the hellhole that is Ruislip Gardens High School. It must be great being an actor and getting to pretend to be someone completely different. How amazing to be able to slip into another life like you're trying on a new outfit or something. I'd give anything to slip into a different life. The trouble is, I don't think I'd want to come back. Well, maybe I would

22

eventually because I'd get worried about my mum and Michaela, but to be someone else for a few hours would be great. But maybe not so great if the scriptwriter decided to electrocute you on a toaster! I wish I had the email addresses for the continuity person and the scriptwriter on Jessop Close. There were so many other ways they could have killed you that would have been way more 'consistent with the previous scene's action' (Television Drama for Dummies). Like coming off your motorbike or falling into the canal or even getting electrocuted by a stun gun in the slaughterhouse. Not that I want you to die of course. As I said to you in my previous email – did you get my previous email? – I feel as if you have died in real life now and I don't know what I'm going to do without having you to watch three times a week. I have made a compilation DVD of your last episodes though. Although I don't think I'll be watching the dreaded 'death by toaster' scene ever again! Can't believe they made your hair stand on end like that, and how did they get all that frothy stuff to come out of your mouth?!!

Anyway, I just wanted you to know that I'm already missing you and I hope you get a new part somewhere soon.

Lots of love,
Your heartbroken fan,
Georgie xxx

From: info@dylancurtland.com
To: georgie*harris@hotmail.com
Date: Mon, 10 July 11:08
Subject: Film Deal

Hi there,

Well, as some of you may have heard, I have been offered my first role in a Hollywood film, and I'm off to LA at the end of the week. Although it is only a minor role I am so excited to have been given this opportunity, and so soon after leaving Jessop Close. The film is the heart-warming true story of a Californian surfer who almost loses his life following a near-fatal jellyfish sting. I play the guy's younger teammate and companion, Chip Daley. I am really looking forward to getting my teeth into the part, and will try to keep you up to date with developments via my website.

Thanks for your continued support and 'have a nice day!'
Dylan x

....

From: georgie*harris@hotmail.com

To: info@dylancurtland.com

Date: Mon, 10 July 16:11

Subject: Re: Film Deal

Dear Dylan,

Am in the library after school and just got your email. My bf Jessica R. Bailey is here too and when I squealed with delight at seeing your new mail in my inbox she came running over (from the health and diet section where she was busy investigating the Zodiac Diet), so I showed her your mail. I thought she'd be really impressed, but she just started laughing. She reckons you haven't been sending the emails at all – she says they're all sent out automatically from your website. I must admit your last email did seem to be addressed to a group of people, like when you say, 'some of you might have heard . . .' but when I showed Jessica your other emails she said they were all automatic emails too. I can't believe that is true. Surely you replied to my first emails personally – didn't you?

Jessica is back in the health section now. If you could see her you'd think she was insane. She's dead skinny but she's always on some diet or other. She says it's preparation for her future modelling career. Personally I couldn't live without food. Well, I guess none of us could live without food, could we, but you know what I mean. How can anyone choose to just eat crab sticks for lunch? Jessica is a Cancer, and Edward Van Trussel, the founder of the Zodiac Diet, says we should all eat food linked to our star signs. To be honest, I think it's a load of old bull and that isn't just because I'm a Taurus! I saw from your birth date on your website that you are an Aquarian and Aquarius is a water carrier, so what are you supposed to live off? A big jug of water? Seriously, how can Jessica believe that rubbish? Her brain is probably in the first stages of starvation. It's probably starting to eat itself it's so hungry! I really shouldn't believe a word she says. So I'm going to continue to believe that you did write me those other emails. Maybe you could send me a more personal reply next time though, so I can prove to Jessica that it is really you and you really are writing to me personally?

Anyway, got to go. My mum said I had to be back by 4.30 because she wants me to take Michaela to the park. Good luck with the film! You must be so excited. It feels weird thinking of you all the way over in America. Thank goodness we still have email to keep in touch.

Lots of love,
Georgie xxx

From: georgie*harris@hotmail.com
To: info@dylancurtland.com
Date: Fri, 21 July 16:25
Subject: Depression

Dear Dylan,

I hope you don't mind me emailing you again but if I don't talk to someone I think I'll go mad. Everything's going really badly wrong at the moment. I feel like the tragic heroine in the black-and-white movie my mum was watching on Saturday afternoon while Tone-Deaf was at the football. Her name was Gracie Delores and she spent the entire film trying to escape from this horrible man with a big black beard and then, when she finally seemed to have lost him, she ended up falling off a cliff, or rather dangling from the top of the cliff and then slowly losing her grip and dropping down lower and lower towards the crashing, foamy waves waiting to sweep her to her doom. 'Oh no, please no!' she kept screaming, but no matter how hard she tried to cling on, the branch would break a bit more, or the cliff face would crumble and down she'd slide. Well that's exactly how I feel right now. No matter how hard I try to make things better they only seem to get worse and worse.

You'd think I'd be happy given that it's the last day of term and I've got the whole summer holiday ahead of me. You'd think I'd be down the park with Jessica and our friends the two Kates, writing graffiti on the shelter and talking about boys, but what's the point? It's all right for the others. They have six weeks of fun to look forward to. Jessica and the two Kates are going to a drama club for three weeks, where they're going to put on a production of Bugsy Malone, but not me. No, Tone-Deaf says I have to stay at home and look after Michaela while he and Angelica are at work. It's so unfair. Why can't he look after her? He's her dad. And he won't even be at work during the day anyway because he always drives his cab at night. So actually I have to look after her while he's asleep or down at the bookies where my mum works. That's how they met by the way – when he went in to put a bet on a race. Why oh why couldn't he have gone to William Hill instead? Then I could have been spared this misery. But then I wouldn't have had Michaela as a sister and that would be equally bad.

You'd love Michaela, everyone does, she is so cute. All rosy cheeks and blonde curls. Not like me with my pale face and dark hair that's so fine it looks like shoelaces. And she says the funniest things too. Yesterday she asked me why teeth don't have eyes so they can see the tooth fairy when she comes for them. She thinks that teeth must get really scared when they're lying there in the darkness under people's pillows (she's obsessed with teeth and the tooth fairy by the way). So I wouldn't want to be without Michaela, but why does her dad have to be so mean? Angelica is always on at me to call him dad, but why should I? I already have a dad, even if he's dead, he's still my dad isn't he? I read this really cool poem once about how people are like stars and just because you can't always see them it doesn't mean they aren't still there. I think my dad is still there, it's just that he hasn't got a way of getting through to me, like a person whose internet connection has gone down or whose mobile phone has run out of credit.

[GEORGIE *gives a dramatic sigh*.]

Sorry, I got the Bugsy Malone script out of the library yesterday and I've been reading it non-stop so I thought I'd put in some stage directions to help you to picture what I'm doing. I hope your film is going well by the way.

Where was I? Oh yes, calling Tone-Deaf my dad. Even if I didn't have a dad, even if I was some kind of miracle kid like Jesus and just had a mum, there is no way I'd call that man Dad. Dads should be loving and kind, shouldn't they? Dads shouldn't shout at you and call you names. Last night he called me a selfish brat because I was upset about not being able to go to the drama workshop. Then he got the compilation DVD I'd made of you and he smashed it up right in front of me, saying I needed to be taught a lesson. What lesson exactly? That it's OK to smash up other people's property? So now I don't even have you to watch anymore, my one escape from the misery that is my life. The worst part is Angelica just stood there while he was doing it. She didn't even try to stop him. Why can't she ever stick up for me? All she ever does is tell me to be quiet, or not to make a fuss. It's like she's scared of him. But I'm not. Honest. I don't care if he's a 6-foot-tall skinhead with a tattoo of an Alsatian on his calf. He's just a bully, and my dad once told me that all bullies are cowards at heart.

I'm sorry if this email is depressing but maybe Jessica's right and you don't even read them anyway. Oh great, now the sign's coming up on the computer telling me I only have one minute left. One minute before I have to return to that hellhole called home.

Yours mournfully,
Georgie x

From: info@dylancurtland.com
To: georgie*harris@hotmail.com
Date: Fri, 21 July 18:19
Subject: Re: Depression

Dear Georgie,

Your dad will always be your dad – and he'll always be alive
in your heart and in your memories and no one but no one
can ever take that away from you. Can I recommend you
read another poem called This Be the Verse by Philip
Larkin. I hope it helps . . .

Dylan x

....

From: georgie*harris@hotmail.com
To: info@dylancurtland.com
Date: Sat, 22 July 10:36
Subject: Wow and thank you!!

Dear Dylan,

OMG!! I am so happy I could kiss the woman sitting at the
computer next to mine. Well maybe not, as she has a bit of

a beard and is sucking a Fisherman's Friend. (Has there ever been a more gross sweet by the way? How can fishermen call them their friends? Mind you, I guess they smell slightly better than fish. Maybe I should buy some for Jessica to suck on after her crab sticks?) Anyway, you emailed me and I can't quite believe it! You actually emailed me and I know for sure it wasn't a group mail. For a start you wrote 'Dear Georgie' instead of 'Hi there', and you talked about my dad too, and you wouldn't talk about my dad in a group email would you? I mean you're hardly going to email all your fans talking about their dead dads are you? For a start, most of their dads wouldn't even be dead and it would be pretty upsetting to receive an email talking about your dad being dead if he wasn't, wouldn't it? But I didn't find your email upsetting at all because it was so true and I hadn't really thought about it like that before. My dad does live on in my heart and my memories, and as long as I think about him and talk to him (in private of course!) then he still exists. And you recommended that great poem especially for me because you knew it would make me feel better. I love the opening line, although, as you know, I don't normally like to swear, but Philip Larkin is so right, Tone-Deaf really does f*** me up. I don't agree with the bit about parents filling you with their faults though. There's no way I'm ever going to bully children or be an ignorant racist like he is. Or have an alcoholic drink. But is life really that grim for everyone? Surely there must be some nice parents out there? My real dad would have never f***ed me up, and if he was still alive my mum would be happy and carefree like she used to be and she wouldn't – well, she wouldn't get so sick either.

What are your parents like? Did they f*** you up too? Is that why you recommended the poem? Sorry, I don't mean to be nosy, but I really hope they aren't anything like Tone-Deaf! Anyway I'd better go now. I left Michaela down in the kids' section looking at the Winnie-the-Pooh books and I can hear her shouting 'Pigwet! Pigwet! Come and eat your honey!' Thank you so much for emailing me and for telling me about the poem. I found it in a compilation of poems called Poems to Rage at Life With and I'm going to get it out right now and read it every time I'm feeling sad and think of you.

Lots of love,
Your friend Georgie x

PS: Can I call you my friend now? In the olden days if we had been writing to each other on paper and stuff we would have been called pen pals. Maybe we could call each other e-mates?

From: info@dylancurtland.com
To: georgie*harris@hotmail.com
Date: Sat, 22 July 14:37
Subject: Re: Wow and thank you!!

Dear Georgie,

Sometimes parents do things that seem selfish and cruel, but the truth is all adults are big kids at heart — just as frightened and vulnerable as the children they boss around. I'm lucky I guess. Like you, I had a wonderful father and my mother really is one of a kind — beautiful, witty and smart. But of course that isn't to say there haven't been tough times along the way. Can I set you a little assignment? I want you to try and work out why Tone-Deaf is the way he is. Think of the Larkin poem and try to find out what his parents were like. What could it be that's making him such an arse?

Your e-mate,
Dylan x

....

From: georgie*harris@hotmail.com
To: info@dylancurtland.com
Date: Sat, 22 July 16:45
Subject: Step-Arses

Dear Dylan,

OMG! Two emails from you in two days! I'm over at Jessica's right now and she's let me use her laptop while she dyes the end of her fringe pink. Jessica has a thing about pink. I'm sitting in her bedroom on the end of her bed and it's like sitting in the middle of a giant marshmallow. Everything from her duvet cover to her carpet to her hairdryer is pink. Even this laptop is pink. I'm scared that if I put it down somewhere I won't be able to find it!

Jessica's going on a date with a boy from Year 10 called Jamie Phelps tonight. Well, not exactly a date, but a party at Jamie's friend Bez's so he is sure to be there and she's hoping something will happen. Jessica has had a crush on Jamie ever since we started at Ruislip Gardens High and apparently last Thursday when she walked past him in the corridor outside the science labs he looked at her and said 'all right', so now she's convinced it's true love! Jamie probably is the nicest looking boy in Ruislip

Gardens – if you like boys that is – personally I prefer men. But anyway, Jessica hasn't told her mum where she's going because her mum doesn't like her going round with older boys – she says they're a bad influence and only interested in one thing. Hmm, I think Jessica's pretty interested in that one thing too. She's always talking about sex (when she isn't talking about the Zodiac Diet that is). Her New Year's resolutions were to lose half a stone and her virginity. Wouldn't it be cool if your virginity was really heavy – then she could achieve two resolutions in one go!

Anyway, her mum thinks she's going to a party at Kate One's. (We go around with two girls called Kate so we have to number them to avoid complications!) Kate One is beautiful – she looks a bit like Cameron Diaz, but the problem is she knows it, if you know what I mean? And Kate Two is a bit more like me. She has dark brown hair too but hers is shorter and really curly.

Right, I'd better hurry up because Jessica will be back in a minute and I don't want her to see your email because – well, it's complicated but she always gets all the attention from the boys in our school and it's nice having something that's just mine for once.

I've been thinking about what you said about parents and stuff and – oh no, I can hear her coming back.

G x

....

From: georgie*harris@hotmail.com
To: info@dylancurtland.com
Date: Mon, 24 July 16:13
Subject: Step-Arses Part Two

Dear Dylan,

Sorry about Saturday – Jessica came racing back into her bedroom freaking out about her hair. She ended up putting a bit too much dye on so instead of just the ends of her fringe being pink the whole thing is! I know this sounds mean but I really wanted to laugh because with her pink fringe and white-blonde hair she looked just like one of those gross crab sticks she keeps eating. I knew I couldn't laugh so I had to think of something really sad to stop me. I always think of the day my dad died when I need to stop laughing and the way my mum's face actually turned grey when she told me about the accident. He was killed in a crash on the motorway. Oh well, at least something good came out of it – at least it's saved me from getting into trouble at school. You see I always have this horrible urge to giggle when I'm getting told off, even though I know it will make things about a billion times worse. But if I think of my dad lying there in the road and his motorbike all mangled up and the blood and . . . well, it's amazing how quickly the laughter disappears. It's a bit like when you spill water on to a hot hob and it all just sizzles away into nothing.

So last night I managed to stop myself laughing and I told Jessica about your emails instead. I know I said I wasn't going to but she was so fed up about her hair I thought it would take her mind off it for a while. I thought she might be excited that you, the world-famous Dylan Curtland, really had emailed me and there was no way it could be spam. The trouble was the whole hair dyeing drama had really traumatised her and she wasn't excited about your new mails at all. In fact she said I was sad for emailing you all the time and I ought to get a life. (You don't think I'm sad, do you? You wouldn't have replied if you did, would you?) Jessica can be a bit like that sometimes. My mum says she's a spoilt little madam but I think it's just because of the stress she's under preparing for her future career as a supermodel. Especially when it goes wrong like last night. She had to cancel going to the party to see Jamie and everything.

Anyway, after I'd made my excuses and gone back home I had a think about what you said in your last email and the assignment you set me about Tone-Deaf's parents. I've only ever met his mum and she seems all right (if you don't mind old ladies who spit and say 'stone me' all the time. And chew toffees non-stop and sit with their legs wide open – while they're wearing a skirt!). I don't know anything about his dad, apart from the fact that he left them when Tone-Deaf was a kid. So I asked my mum about him when we were giving Michaela her bath last night and Mum said that he used to beat Tone-Deaf and his brothers and that's why they don't have anything to do with him any more. She also said Tone-Deaf had a lot of 'unresolved anger issues' and that's why she sometimes tells me to be quiet because she's scared he might lose his temper with me. I wanted to say to her that it didn't seem very fair that he could get mad at me because of what his dad did – but my mum was having a really good day. She had put on George Michael's Greatest Hits and was singing and dancing around the bathroom to Club Tropicana, so I just left it.

Then, when Tone-Deaf got back from the football, I made him a cup of tea and a sausage sandwich with brown sauce on the top and mustard on the bottom just how he likes it, and I gave him the remote control straight away, even though I'd been watching a really funny old episode of

Friends. Maybe if I'm nice to him I can get him to change? And then it won't be like Philip Larkin's poem at all because he'll stop handing his misery on to me and I can be nothing but joyful with my own kids?

Oh, that was another thing I wanted to say. Why did you write 'I HAD a wonderful father'? Is your dad dead too? If he is, isn't that a weird coincidence? Your mum sounds really nice – and just like mine. Well, mine is definitely beautiful and she can be witty. I'm not so sure about smart though lol! (Although I didn't actually laugh out loud because I'm in the library and you have to be dead quiet in here.)

Oh well, better take Michaela to feed the ducks, she keeps hitting me on the leg and the cross-eyed librarian with the hunchback is glaring at us – well at least I think she is . . . Hope the film is going OK.

[GEORGIE *sits back in her chair and pinches herself to make sure she isn't dreaming and she really is emailing the world-famous actor Dylan Curtland!*]

Lots of love,
Your e-mate Georgie xxx

From: info@dylancurtland.com
To: georgie*harris@hotmail.com
Date: Mon, 24 July 20:06
Subject: Crabby Friends

Dear Georgie,

Ask yourself who is sadder – the girl who writes fascinating emails to her new friend or the girl who looks just like a walking crab stick? One time, when a journalist at a tabloid had written something really insulting about my acting, my mum gave me some really cool – or should I say 'frost-free' – advice. She told me that whenever someone hurls an insult at you, you should boomerang it straight back at them and ask what it is that makes them need to demean you?

Dylan x

....

From: georgie*harris@hotmail.com
To: info@dylancurtland.com
Date: Tue, 25 July 11:10
Subject: Re: Crabby Friends

Dear Dylan,

I can't believe you said 'frost-free'! That is so frost-free. And your mum sounds really frost-free too. With that boomerang thing, do you mean like Tone-Deaf being angry at his dad and then taking it out on me, because it really isn't like that for Jessica. Her parents are lovely and give her everything she wants and I've never, ever heard them get mad at her, even when she answers them back. Her mum is one of those parents who always hovers around in the background like a little hummingbird, offering drinks of Sunny Delight and help with homework and lifts to places and making sure everything is just fine. And her dad is called Gregory and he has this big black briefcase and he's always talking on his mobile phone in a very important voice. They are like the parents you would get in the advert for Perfect Parents R Us – if there was such a thing as a store for perfect parents. So you see Jessica really doesn't have any reason to be f***ed up. I think the other day she was just stressed out about her hair, I don't think she 'needs' to demean me. Usually she's really nice to me – she always makes me sit

42

with her in the canteen or on the bus and she says I'm the only person who really knows what she goes through and the burden she has to carry, the only person she can really trust. Back when we were 11 we even tried to become blood sisters but we only had a pair of nail scissors and they were too blunt, so we became toenail sisters instead (I still have her toenail clipping inside my locket, along with a tiny picture of my dad smoking a cigarette on Blackpool Pier).

Thank you for your advice though – and for saying my emails are fascinating! Are they really? Sometimes I wonder if you think I'm a right mentalist because I write exactly what I'm thinking, the way I'm thinking, and I don't know if it even makes sense, but thank you! I think your emails are fascinating too – not just because they're from you but the things you say. You sound so wise and so different from your character on Jessop Close. Not that Jimmy was stupid or anything but you do sound different – more grown up – but that's fine.

I am so glad I have you as an e-mate and can tell you these things. I can't believe any journalist would insult your acting though! I call those sort of papers the taborrhoids (a mixture of tabloids and haemorrhoids) because they are full of crap and painful to read lolsil (laughing out loud silently in library). Tone-Deaf has haemorrhoids by the way – I saw his ointment in the bathroom cabinet. Sometimes when he's mean to me I remind myself of the list of symptoms on the packet and it makes me feel a bit better imagining him going through all that. He always buys the taborrhoids too and spends ages looking at the topless women, even when my mum is there. I think he likes making her feel insecure because when she asks him to stop he just laughs and says things like, 'What – jealous because she's a real woman?' I don't understand what he's going on about because my mum is definitely a real woman – and she's beautiful too. You would love her if you could see – she has these huge slate-grey eyes with long, long lashes and really dark hair but it's thicker than mine and prettier because it's like silk rather than clumps of string! I think those women in the paper look like Barbie dolls whose chests have been blown up with a bicycle pump. Angelica doesn't even need make-up to look good – unless she's had one of her funny turns – then her eyes go all red and she looks a bit too pale. I wish she wasn't married to Tone-Deaf – I'm sure he's what makes her get ill. But anyway I mustn't start being mean about Tone-Deaf again because I'm trying to turn over a new leaf and be nicer to him because then he might let me go to the drama workshop next week.

I'm supposed to be taking Michaela to the park now but I'm dreading it in case any of my mates are there. Don't get me wrong, I really love Michaela, but what if my friends are all hanging out at the pavilion and I've got to push her on the swings or play Tiggers with her? I hate always being the odd one out. I'm the only one who hasn't got a mobile phone or a computer because Tone-Deaf is too tight to buy me one, so I always miss out on all the messaging and stuff. One time Jamie Phelps was online and someone messaged him pretending to be Jessica. I won't tell you what they said but it was really gross and involved animals and Jessica went mad when she found out. She said she was going to hunt down whoever did it and 'rip off their head and stuff their computer keyboard down the hole!!' Hmm – maybe it's not such a bad thing not being online – at least no one can pretend to be me because everyone knows I haven't got a PC.

Sorry, I've been rambling on again. I don't know what happens when I start writing to you – it's like someone turns on a tap in my brain and all my thoughts come flooding out on to the keyboard. So what is it like in Hollywood? It said in Tone-Deaf's taborrhoid the other day that all the stars over there are going crazy about the Zodiac Diet. I hope you aren't, especially as you are an Aquarius. If your film producers try and make you go on it why don't you lie and say you are an Aries or something? At least then you won't have to live off water and you can eat some meat –

although I'm not sure if ram tastes all that good!

Anyway, I hope it's going well and you've learnt all your lines. Oh God, I hope I can persuade Tone-Deaf to let me go to the drama workshop next week – then we could compare notes about our different productions. Have you ever been in Bugsy Malone?

Lots of love,
Your e-mate Georgie xx

....

From: georgie*harris@hotmail.com
To: info@dylancurtland.com
Date: Wed, 26 July 14:22
Subject: Worst nightmares!!

Dear Dylan,

Just wanted to update you on my worst nightmare coming true yesterday. Well actually it wasn't my WORST nightmare – that would be being stuck on a desert island forever with Tone-Deaf – but it came pretty close. As I said in my previous email (please don't worry about replying to every single one of my mails – I know you are mega busy right now) anyway, as I said, yesterday I took Michaela to the park and yes, as predicted, all of my mates were there. And not only that but Jamie Phelps and two of his mates were there too. The minute I spotted them on the pavilion I hurried over to the kids' play area pretending I hadn't seen them. I even did a different kind of walk so they wouldn't recognise me – a kind of limp with my head bowed right down. Then I wondered why a person might limp with their head bowed down and I decided that I was actually a Swedish au pair who had fallen off her pony just before she came to England to work. Then I decided that she would have had a pony because she was from a very rich family, perhaps even royalty, if they have royalty in Sweden, but the reason I was an au pair was because I loved children so much and I wanted to see what it was like in the real world before I became queen. That way I would be a totally frost-free queen because I'd understand what it was like to be poor and I wouldn't be a parasite. My dad used to say that all of the Royal Family are parasites because they live off the rest of us. I wasn't exactly sure what he meant to be honest but it got me into loads of trouble in biology a couple of years ago when Mr Connor asked us for an example of a parasite and I said the Queen. He put me in detention and I had to write a 500-word essay entitled 'What the Royal Family Has Done for Me'. I thought about leaving the page blank – that's what my dad would have wanted me to do. He would have laughed his roaring laugh and given me one of his bear hugs if I'd done that – and if he'd been alive of course. In the end I wrote a page on how nice Prince Harry's smile is and about half a page on how good it is that the Royal Family give football fans something to sing about. (The truth is I hate it when Tone-Deaf sings the National Anthem, he sounds like a monotonous moron – we've been doing alliteration in English by the way.) But anyway Mr Connor seemed to like it – well, he let me out of detention and told me I needed to 'curb my imagination'. Hmm – I felt like saying he needed to try and FIND his imagination but obviously I didn't dare, so I just thought it instead.

Where was I? Oh yes, the park. If only I could forget the whole sorry episode and wipe it from my memory. So I walked, or rather limped, over to the swings pretending to be Princess Pippi (after Pippi Longstocking – I think she was Swedish and she was my hero when I was a kid. Imagine living in a house with just a monkey and a horse and, more importantly, no annoying grown-ups who bellow about saving the Queen and then perv over women in the newspaper!). And just as I got there I heard Jessica shout out, 'George!' I knew it was Jessica because she's the only person who calls me George rather than Georgie and she's just started talking with a bit of an American accent.

Apparently, when she was three, she lived in America with her parents for a year – her dad works for a bank and they have an office in New York. Jessica says when she was learning to talk she was surrounded by Americans and that is why she speaks with a bit of a drawl. But the weird thing is she never used to. Up until about a month ago she had a posh London accent! Anyway she kept shouting to me over and over again until Michaela noticed and started shouting back at her. Michaela loves Jessica, she thinks she looks just like one of the princesses in her comic, it must be all the pink clothes and blonde hair. Do you prefer blondes by the way? My mum loves this old film called Gentlemen Prefer Blondes. I don't know why she likes it because she's got dark hair! Anyway, I told Michaela not to shout back but she just ignored me and kept waving and shrieking 'Jess! Jess!' So then I had to wave at them too and then they called me over and so I had no choice, I had to go over because otherwise it would look like I was blanking them, and of course I had to keep limping or it would have looked really weird. Trust me, it was a very noticeable limp so I couldn't just lose it. I'm going to write the next bit in script format so you can picture the whole humiliating scene as if it was in a film:

[JESSICA R. BAILEY, KATE ONE, KATE TWO, JAMIE PHELPS *and* TWO EQUALLY COOL YOUNG MEN *are* sat on the pavilion of Ruislip Gardens Park. The sun is shining and the sound of birds chirping and children playing fills the air. GEORGIE HARRIS enters limping and holding her cute little half sister MICHAELA by the hand.]

GEORGIE: [looking at the ground] All right?

MICHAELA: Jess! Jess!

GEORGIE: Shhh!

JESSICA: [in slight American drawl] Hi Michaela. [To KATE ONE and KATE TWO] Aw, isn't she cute? [To GEORGIE] What's up with your leg?

[GEORGIE pretends not to hear.]

JESSICA: [louder] George? What's up with your leg? Why are you limping?

[GEORGIE starts to blush and doesn't know what she hates the most – the way her cheeks always burn at the slightest thing or the way JESSICA always calls her George like she's a boy.]

GEORGIE: Nothing. I – er – fell over.

MICHAELA: No you didn't.

GEORGIE: [glaring at her 'cute' little sister] I did, you just didn't see me do it.

MICHAELA: Can you play on the swing with me, Jess?

JESSICA: Sorry, honey, we're going to the movies in a minute. Can you come, George or do you have to [looks pointedly at MICHAELA] look after you-know-who?

GEORGIE: [shaking head woefully] Sorry.

[JAMIE *gets up and moves towards* GEORGIE, *he is holding a guitar case.*]

JAMIE: Right – I'm off.

JESSICA: Have a good session. [*She giggles and lowers her head.*]

JAMIE: [*hoisting guitar over shoulder*] Yeah, thanks. [*To* GEORGIE *as he passes her*] See ya.

[GEORGIE *blushes even redder.*]

JESSICA: [*frowning*] Don't forget the drama workshop on Monday, Jamie – they really need someone who can sing as well as you. You'd get the part of Bugsy easy.

JAMIE: Yeah – maybe.

[JAMIE *exits park left.* EQUALLY COOL YOUNG MEN *start having a burping contest.*]

JESSICA: [*frowning as she stares after* JAMIE] Do you know if you can come to the drama workshop yet, George?

GEORGIE: Yes – yes I can – definitely . . .

[*Fades . . .*]

I know, I know, I shouldn't have lied, but the thing is I want to go to the workshop so badly – even more now I've read the Bugsy Malone script. I'd love to get a part like Blousey or Tallulah! Of course I would never in a million years get a part like that. I've never once had the main part in a school play, I always have to play a sheep or hold up a card with a random word on it, and one year, when we were doing

51

A Christmas Carol I had to be a snowflake! So I'd probably only get Girl Number Three in Bugsy Malone – or even worse, Undertaker Number One! But just to be involved would be so frost-free and then you could give me tips – if you had the time of course – and I would be the best undertaker the world has ever seen!

On Oprah the other day this lady was talking about her new book called Dream It, Live It, Be It and she said that the best way to make your dreams come true is to act as if they already have. So hopefully by telling Jessica I can come to the workshop I will somehow miraculously be able to go. Maybe Tone-Deaf will get a personality transplant surgeon in the back of his cab tonight and he'll give him the operation for free and make him be really nice and kind and care about his stepdaughter's happiness lolsil! I know you say on your website that the things you hate most in life are baked beans and dishonesty, but I honestly don't normally tell lies, I was just embarrassed that's all. I didn't want to have to tell Jessica I couldn't come to the workshop until I absolutely knew it for sure. I hope you understand and don't think badly of me?

Oh well, I'm going to go back home now and see if Tone-Deaf wants me to do any jobs round the house – and while I'm doing them I'm going to dream that I've been given a totally frost-free part in Bugsy Malone and my acting is half as good as yours (because then it would be truly, truly great).

Your dreaming, living, being it e-mate,
Georgie xxx

....

From: info@dylancurtland.com
To: georgie*harris@hotmail.com
Date: Wed, 26 July 17:32
Subject: Confession

Dear Georgie,

Well – where to begin? Your emails certainly are 'full'! Perhaps honesty would be a good place to start as it's where you left off.

You see, I haven't exactly been straight with you. I had thought that my dishonesty was harmless enough but when you expressed such concern that I should trust you in your last mail – well – I felt a complete and utter hypocrite. So here goes – confession time. You see I'm not Dylan – never have been. I feel terrible because I know you care a great deal for Dylan but he's been so busy lately that he just hasn't had the time to handle his correspondence, so he put me in charge of it. And the thing is, normally I do just send out standard emails: thank you mails, acknowledgements, that type of thing. Your friend was right I'm afraid, those first emails I sent to you were standard responses. But your emails were so lively and interesting and your stories about your stepfather got me so mad I had to email you back personally. And I guess I thought it wouldn't hurt to carry on pretending to be Dylan because I knew that would mean a lot to you – and trust me, if Dylan had read your emails he would have wanted me to say all the things I did. But when I read your last two emails I knew I had to come clean. I felt terrible reading that you were worried about what I – or rather Dylan – might think of your own, completely understandable, lie, whilst all the time I had been deceiving you.

So, for the truth. My name is Nancy Curtland – or Nan to my friends, of whom, if you can find it in your heart to forgive me, I hope you will become one? And I am Dylan's mother. I live with my cocker spaniel, Woodstock, in a beachside house in a place called Hove, near Brighton. My husband, and Dylan's father, Bruce, died late last year, so when I wrote to you about your father I really meant what

I said, I really can appreciate your loss. What else? I have silver hair (don't you just hate the word grey – so dreary and grim sounding?) and my hairdresser friend Mario has just cut it into a choppy little bob. He says it makes me look ten years younger, which at my age, trust me, makes one hell of a difference.

Oh, Georgie, I feel so terrible about what I have done and I hope you aren't too disappointed to discover that your 'e-mate' is just some stupid lonely old woman rather than a 'Hollywood heart-throb.' I have really enjoyed receiving your emails and the truth is I don't want you to stop writing to me. Well actually I guess I want you to *start* writing to me – now that you know the truth and know who I am. However, I will completely understand if you don't and I never hear from you again – I fear I have behaved appallingly.

Yours shamefacedly,
Nan x

....

Part Two

Ordinary Fool

From: georgie*harris@hotmail.com
To: info@dylancurtland.com
Date: Fri, 28 July 10:16
Subject: Re: Confession

Dear Ms Curtland,

Thank you for your email. Unfortunately I don't think it will be possible for us to continue to be e-mates. I hope you understand.

Yours sincerely,
Georgie Harris.

....

From: georgie*harris@hotmail.com
To: info@dylancurtland.com
Date: Fri, 28 July 10:25
Subject: Re: Confession

How could you? I really trusted you. I really thought you were Dylan. Do you have any idea how happy that made me feel — that Dylan Curtland was actually emailing me? That for once in my pathetic life something really cool was happening to me? That for the first time since my dad died someone was making me feel special again. And for the first time I didn't mind feeling different from everyone else because for the first time I had something the other girls would be jealous of rather than the other way round? Now I feel even worse than I did before because I feel so STUPID!!! Jessica is so going to love this when she finds out. Why couldn't you have just been honest with me from the start or not bothered emailing me at all? I don't understand why you would do something like that. Was it so you could make fun of me? I might not be a famous actor but I am a person and I do have feelings and right now I feel so embarrassed thinking about all the stuff I said in my mails, thinking that you were Dylan.

From: georgie*harris@hotmail.com
To: info@dylancurtland.com
Date: Fri, 28 July 10:27
Subject: Re: Confession

And what about the stuff you said in your emails? I just had another look at them. What about the one where you say, 'My mother really is one of a kind – beautiful, witty and smart'?!! Well, you can add mean and dishonest to that list too!

....

From: georgie*harris@hotmail.com
To: info@dylancurtland.com
Date: Fri, 28 July 11:42
Subject: Sorry – a bit

Dear Ms Curtland,

I apologise for my previous emails – I took Michaela to the pet shop to see the baby hamsters and looking at their cute little cheeks and the way they stuff them up so full gave me a chance to calm down. I was so angry and embarrassed before. I didn't mean to be rude, it's just that I was really disappointed to find out you weren't Dylan. I'm sure you're probably a very nice person, but I don't know you and it's not just your messages but it's what they made me do that is so embarrassing. Like lying in bed every night imagining Dylan typing those emails to me and wondering if he was replying to my latest one right there and then and then some nights (OK, most nights) I would also imagine him actually saying all that stuff to me in person too. Like over an intimate corner table in a coffee bar or walking along that dead famous road with the arch in Paris or in Ruislip Gardens bus shelter. That's why I feel so stupid, because the best thing to have happened to me in ages was all just a lie. Oh, this is so hard to explain!

OK, imagine you saw a homeless man sitting in a doorway and he had flies buzzing all round his head and dirt and grime smeared on his face and everything, but you didn't rush past him like everyone else, you stopped and you talked to him and then you told him that it was all going to be OK because you had loads of money and loads of houses and you were going to give him a house and some money so he could sort himself out and his life was never going to be rubbish again. Imagine how happy he'd feel and how he'd get up from his grotty doorway and he'd go skipping down the road to the address you'd given him, singing happy songs like that really annoying one from the Wizard of Oz, at the top of his voice, but then, when he got there, he found out that it was just an old building site and there was no house and there was no money after all. Imagine how terrible he'd feel – even worse than before because at least before he didn't have any hope. But you did the worst possible thing because you gave him hope and then you took it away. Well, that's how I feel. All that time thinking that Dylan was actually – well anyway – I just wanted you to know how I feel.

I've got to go now because I promised my mum I would have got the cleaning done by the time she gets back from work and so far I've only done the bedrooms.

Yours sincerely,
Georgie Harris.

....

From: info@dylancurtland.com
To: georgie*harris@hotmail.com
Date: Fri, 28 July 15:42
Subject: Re: Sorry – a bit

Dear Georgie,

Well, I've been compared to some things in my time but an old building site really does beat the lot of them hands down. I am so terribly sorry. The trouble is I never think my actions through before I make them. But I always have the best of intentions, I promise you. Let me give you an example.

Back when I was a young girl, so long ago now I can hardly bear contemplate, I fancied myself as a bit of a cupid. If I had friends who were single I saw it as my duty to pair them up with a suitable beau. The problem was I was so set upon fixing them up I sometimes paid little heed to the 'suitable' part of the arrangement. One summer, my very best friend at the time, a girl called Anna, who liked eating bananas dipped in jam and bore more than a passing resemblance to a rabbit (she had the most enormous eyes, rather over-sized front teeth and pale, fur-like hair on the sides of her cheeks), was desperate to meet her soulmate. Every day during that summer holiday she would come over to my house and we would talk for hours about the lack of decent boys in our village and she would fling herself on my bed and wail about never finding true love. Well, for a frustrated cupid like me it was too good an opportunity to miss, and as luck would have it a new boy had just come to work on my father's farm. His name was Cyril, but I didn't hold that against him, and he was employed to help out in the dairy. Apart from his name and the rather unfortunate manner in which he would start frothing at the mouth when excited, he seemed like the perfect match for my poor, love-thirsty friend. So I organised a game of sardines. I don't know if your generation ever play sardines? Basically it's like hide-and-seek but only one person hides and then all the others have to try to find them, and when they do, they have to hide with them until everyone is squashed into the hiding place like 'sardines' and only one person is left seeking. This poor unfortunate is then declared 'out'. So, one Sunday when Cyril had finished his shift in the dairy and Anna and I were loitering about by the gate to the yard, I called him over and suggested we play the game. I let Anna hide first, knowing full well she would choose her usual place in the coal bunker around the side of the house, then I watched as Cyril set about trying to find her. The wretched boy took hours to figure it out, but finally he crawled into the bunker and I ran over and bolted the door behind him. You see, I thought that if they were tragically trapped together love was bound to bloom, as they clung together for warmth and comfort etc, etc.

Unfortunately however, the only thing to bloom in that coal bunker was mass hysteria. It turned out that amongst Cyril's many afflictions he was also claustrophobic. As soon as he realised he was trapped, rather than begin to seduce Anna as I had planned, he began to scream. And scream and scream. Unfortunately I didn't hear him as I had gone into the house in order to allow love to bloom and to have a bowl of ice cream – all that chasing around pretending to look for Anna had worked up a ferocious appetite. I'm not sure exactly how long I left them there. Anna said it was half a day. I would guess at half an hour, but when I did venture back to unbolt the door all merry hell broke loose. Cyril burst out of that bunker like a bull at a gate, streams of saliva and coal dust streaking his face and his hair practically standing on end. We quite literally didn't see him for dust as he fled the farm. Anna was furious, yelling at me for being so stupid and demanding to know what I had been thinking. Even when I tried to explain that I'd done it all for her and the course of true love she still wouldn't calm down. And now, with the benefit of hindsight, I can see that she was completely right. What on earth had I been thinking locking her in there with a boy who foamed at the mouth and had a name that rhymed with squirrel? I should have shut her in there with one of the stable-hands, they were way better looking and far hardier.

So you see, Georgie, ever since I was a child I've had a terrible knack of doing the wrong thing, but never for the wrong reason. Now, I realise only too well why my pretending to be Dylan could only end in heartache, but I honestly only ever wrote to you to try to make you feel happier, and I can assure you it was never to make fun of you. You are a fascinating person and your emails are so full of zest – I had really started looking forward to getting the latest updates from your world.

Speaking of which – I do so hope you are able to go to the Bugsy Malone workshop next week. Back before I had Dylan I dabbled a little in the theatre world and one of my first ever roles was Blousey. I will keep everything crossed for you – apart from my eyes because that really isn't a good look, especially at my age. I don't want to get carted off to the funny farm with suspected dementia!

Good luck, Georgie, in all that you do, and remember, you don't stay a child forever. One day you will be free from Tone-Deaf and you will have the whole world at your feet. One day you won't have to ask anyone's permission to do anything. Keep holding out for that day — it comes soon enough.

Nan xx

....

From: georgie*harris@hotmail.com
To: info@dylancurtland.com
Date: Sat, 29 July 11.01
Subject: OK

Dear Nan,

It sounds funny writing 'Dear Nan' — as if I'm writing to my grandma or something. Not that that would be possible as I'm not in touch with either of my real nans. I'm not allowed to speak to my dad's mum. Tone-Deaf says that his mum's my nan now — and my mum hasn't seen her parents since she ran away to be with my dad. It was dead romantic how my mum and dad met. Angelica was only 16 and she had gone to see this really cool band called the Magic Carpets in Manchester, where she comes from. At the end of the concert she and her friends tried to get backstage to meet the band and that's how she met Jeff, my dad. He wasn't in

68

the band, he was one of their roadies. (Roadies are the ones who move all the instruments and stuff when a band are on tour and they set it all up for the gigs. They have to be dead strong.) I think that's probably why my mum fell in love with Dad straight away, because she knew he would look after her. He wasn't as tall as Tone-Deaf and he didn't have a skinhead or tattoos or anything, but he was way stronger.

There are different kinds of strength aren't there? There are muscles and shouty voices and shaven heads, but that isn't real strength, that's just a wrapping. Real strength comes from the inside, like the writing running through a stick of rock. My dad was calm and funny and wise and he had strength running right through him and Angelica never left him after that first night. Don't you think that's romantic — to just meet someone and know instantly that they're the one for you? I love getting my mum to tell me the story of how they met and how she went back to his hotel room that night and he played his guitar to her for hours and hours and sang her this song called Wonderful Tonight by Eric Clapton and it made her cry. Not because she was sad but because she was happy because she knew she wouldn't ever have to go back home again. Before she met my dad, my mum had lain in bed every night dreaming of the day that someone would come and rescue her, but in her dreams she was never able to see his face. As soon as she saw my dad she knew it was him. She thought she must have dreamt about him so much she'd made him come to life.

I love it when she tells me that bit – it makes me go all shivery down the back of my neck and I think it's the same for her too because she always gets this far away look in her eyes and her voice goes all whispery. It's a bit like that book that they were talking about on Oprah, isn't it, Dream it, Live It, Be It? Angelica's parents were really mean to her – much, much worse than Tone-Deaf. They used to lock her in her bedroom and hit her with a leather belt just for doing things like talking to the boy who delivered the papers or not eating her cauliflower. How could you hit anyone for not eating cauliflower? I'd want to shake their hand! Anyway my mum stayed with Jeff from that moment on, travelling around with him and the band and living with him in his flat in this place in London called Kilburn. That was where I was born, about a year after they met. So my mum was only a few years older than I am now when she had me. I can't imagine having a kid of my own, although I guess I've learnt a lot about what it must be like from Michaela. I certainly know how to change a nappy and tell a bedtime story, that's for sure!

I googled you. I hope you don't mind? It was just that after everything that's happened recently I wanted to make sure you really did exist and weren't someone pretending to be someone pretending to be Dylan! You've acted in loads of things haven't you? I found an article on the Times newspaper website about you and Dylan's dad. He looked really nice. I'm so sorry he got cancer. It sounded really romantic how you met when he directed you in that play. Oh God, I hope I meet my soulmate in a dead romantic way too. You did and my mum did, so I know it's possible. But then my mum also met Tone-Deaf in a bookies, so the path of true love can go badly wrong sometimes can't it? In the photo on the Times website your husband looked so gentle and kind. And you looked really beautiful. I love your hair. It was so long and shiny. Can you give me any tips on getting shiny hair? Mine always looks as dull as mud – even worse than grey! But I bet your hair looks really nice now it's silver and in a bob. Bobs are all the rage at the moment, aren't they? Jessica refuses to get one because she read in Vogue that 'successful supermodels are never slaves to fashion, but set their own trends.'

Your husband Bruce had really twinkly eyes, just like my dad's. I bet he was a nice director. I wonder what the director of Bugsy Malone will be like. I've got a cunning plan about the drama workshop by the way. I went to the community centre today and gave in my form and on Monday I'm going to take Michaela along and ask if she can just sit quietly at the back of the hall and watch. She's a really good kid, she never has tantrums or throws toys around or anything and I'm sure if I promise to buy her a new Tigger I can get her to keep quiet to my mum and Tone-Deaf.

As you can probably guess, I've decided to forgive you. You sound really nice in your emails, even when you're not pretending to be Dylan. And you've given me some really frost-free advice. I'm glad you like getting my emails too, though I can't see why you would find me 'fascinating'. My life feels so dreary and dull compared to yours, my days are all grey for sure.

Can I ask you something? Is Dylan like the character he played in Jessop Close in real life? As you know from my first email to him [GEORGIE *blushes redder than a STOP sign at the excruciating memory!*] I used to love watching him play Jimmy and he played him so well. Is he like that at home too? I don't mean all the angry stuff – I really hope he doesn't shout at you the way he did to Maureen!! But is he sensitive and kind – and does he play the guitar?

Thank you for your last email and for keeping everything apart from your eyes crossed for me. Hope you approve of my cunning plan and I'll let you know how I get on. I can't believe you played Blousey, that is like the best part in the whole play!!

Your e-mate,
Georgie xx

....

From: nancyblue#@aol.com
To: georgie*harris@hotmail.com
Date: Sun, 30 July 10:06
Subject: You Go Girl!!

Dear Georgie,

Atta girl! I'm so pleased you are going to go to the workshop. And SO, SO pleased you still want to be e-mates. As you will see from above, I've emailed you from my own personal address this time. It seemed to make more sense, now we are proper e-mates?

Now – re your questions. Of course I don't mind you googling me. That term always makes me giggle. I have a friend called Ricardo – an extremely camp choreographer with a TinTin quiff and a chronic lisp – and he always says, 'Girl, you ain't arrived till you've been googled!' So now I

73

can tell him with pride that I've been googled with the best of them. My husband Bruce is – was (don't you just hate the word 'was' – it's so damned final) – a lovely man and you were quite right, he was gentler and kinder than any man I've ever met, and an absolute joy as a director. Your story of how your parents met brought tears to my eyes because it was so reminiscent of Bruce's and my first meeting. I was a lot older than your mother when we met though – nearly 40 – and I'd certainly kissed a lot of frogs by then! But it was well worth the wait believe me. And like your mother, I just knew, the moment I laid eyes on him, that he was the one for me. So don't worry, Georgie – if you believe they will happen badly enough, your dreams will indeed come true, exactly like that book on the Oprah show.

I wonder how many women lie in bed at night dreaming of a man to come and rescue them. Imagine if, in all the beds across the land, heart-shaped, cartoon dream bubbles are drifting from women's heads as they toss and turn and hug their tear-stained pillows. It seems such a tragedy that even in this day and age women should still feel trapped. But don't worry, Georgie, as I said in my last email, your time will come, and once you taste that freedom there'll be no stopping you. Your days might seem grey right now but I can tell from your emails that your mind is a kaleidoscope of colour and that is what counts, believe me.

You asked about Dylan being like Jimmy and the answer is yes and no. Yes he is sensitive and kind – takes after his father there thankfully – but he is also a bit of a free spirit with a tendency to overdramatise somewhat. Can't think where he gets that from!! But all in all he is a lovely boy and I am very, very proud of what he is doing right now. Although I have to say the house feels quieter than a morgue with both him and Bruce gone. Still, at least I have my trusty dog Woodstock and my new e-mate to keep me company. Dylan doesn't play the guitar at all by the way, they had to have a guitar-playing double for those scenes in his bedroom when he played the blues.

Good luck at the drama workshop tomorrow. I guess you might not get this email until after you've been so I hope it goes well and I hope they let you bring your sister. I'm off to Sunday lunch with a couple of friends shortly. We do it every last Sunday of the month, but to be honest with you I'd really rather we didn't any more. It was something we started when Bruce was alive. The four of us would go to a lovely old pub on the Sussex Downs called The Snowdrop, where they have an open fire and proper home-made food and the landlord calls you 'lover'. Although I have to say that is not the most appealing of prospects, his humungous backside spills over his waistband like rising bread in a loaf tin. I used to love our lazy Sundays there, but now it is quite unbearable sitting next to an empty chair, all the time wishing that the next time I look up I will see Bruce striding back from the toilet or the bar and the past nine months will have all been a bad dream. Still, you have to make an effort, don't you? And I know my friends are only trying to look out for me. So I'll go and put on a brave face and try not to let it get to me. The show must go on and all that jazz.

Anyway, enough of this self-pitying ramble. There's something very seductive about this emailing lark, isn't there? The way the words just seem to tumble out on to the screen. Far more relaxed and free-flowing than writing a letter. Bruce never approved of the internet – he thought it stopped people from properly interacting. But without email how would you and I have ever got talking? And I'm sure neither of us would have been able to be so frank with each other if we'd met face to face.

Let me know how you get on tomorrow Georgie, and if you do read this before you go, BREAK A LEG, darling!

Your e-mate,
Nan xx

....

From: nancyblue#@aol.com
To: georgie*harris@hotmail.com
Date: Sun, 30 July 10:22
Subject: PS

Top tip for hair that gleams like diamonds – comb some olive oil through it before going to bed (around half a cupful should suffice, depending on length of hair) then wash it out in the morning. Never fails!

Nx

....

From: georgie*harris@hotmail.com
To: nancyblue#@aol.com
Date: Mon, 31 July 16:27
Subject: OMG!

Dear Nan,

OH! MY! GOD! I went to the drama workshop today and it was great! OK, I need to take a deep breath and pull myself together because I only have half an hour booked on the computer because I really have to get home because I promised my mum I'd have the vegetables peeled before she got home from work. And Michaela is starving so I'm not sure how long she'll stay in the kids' section without yelling for some Jelly Babies.

This morning I got up at about 8 and had some breakfast with my mum before she left for work and I asked her one last time if I could go to the workshop. I really don't know what the big deal is – it's run by the council so it's totally free. But as usual she said no because Tone-Deaf had to sleep when he got home from work and who else was going to look after Michaela? Part of me wanted to slam my toast down and say, 'How about one of Michaela's parents?' But I didn't because Angelica looked so pale and tired and I know it isn't really her fault. I know she doesn't even want to work. One morning in the Easter holidays I found her sitting on the end of her bed in her betting shop uniform really crying. All her mascara had run down her face in long black streaks and she kept rocking backwards and forwards holding on to her knees, even when I cuddled her. When I asked her what was wrong she said she wished she didn't have to work such long hours because she never got to have any fun with me and Michaela. Then, when I asked her why she didn't just give up her job or work part-time at least, like she used to when I was little, she said she couldn't because she needed to pay her share of the mortgage. And although she didn't say it, I knew she meant my share of the mortgage too because one night I'd heard her and Tone-Deaf arguing and he shouted, 'If you and your daughter want to live here then you have to pay your way.' Bastard! Sorry – I hope you don't mind me swearing? I know Dylan doesn't like girls who swear but maybe you can understand that sometimes girls just have to swear. Especially when they have a stepdad like Tone-Deaf! I know he meant me when he said 'your daughter', even though Michaela is mum's daughter too. Because Michaela is 'theirs', isn't she? Not just 'hers' like I am.

Sometimes I see the way he looks at me (the same way he looks at northerners and asylum seekers) and I know he really hates me because I'm not his. He's so different with Michaela. He calls her his princess and lets her sit on his knee and he always buys her presents. But I suppose I'm luckier than Michaela in a way because at least when I was four my mum would be at home in the holidays and after school. And she was much more fun then too. She never got ill and would always be dancing and singing about the place and making up games in her head. I loved her games. She could make anything seem fun back then. Even trips to the dentist – which I hate by the way. Angelica knew I got really scared so she would pretend that we were spies and we had to collect information about all the people in the waiting room. It was so cool. I hardly got scared at all then. I was too busy trying to figure out why the old lady sitting opposite me was knitting a scarf. Was she actually knitting a deadly weapon to strangle someone with? Or why the man sitting next to me had a briefcase on his lap. Was he about to drop off some top-secret information to another secret agent? By the time I got in to see the dentist my head was so busy unravelling mysteries I didn't get too bothered by the drill or that horrible scraper thing. Sometimes I try and play my mum's old games with Michaela but it never feels the same, they never seem as fun. It's a bit like orange squash. My mum's games were like the squash when it's all bright and strong and still in the bottle, but when I try and play them it's like they've been watered down. Was that a good simile by the way? Similes are one of my targets in English.

Thank you for saying that nice stuff about my imagination. I liked your kaleidoscope metaphor. If my imagination is like a kaleidoscope of colour then my mum's imagination used to be like a fireworks display, it was so bright and exciting. But not any more. Now it's like the fireworks have got all soggy and wet and it's impossible to even get a spark out of them. Like Tone-Deaf came along and poured a big old bucket of water all over them. So you see there was no point arguing with her this morning because I'd only have made her even more depressed. Oh no – I can see Michaela coming – hold on, I'll just give her some Jelly Babies.

OK, I really have to rush now, the clock on the computer is telling me I only have ten minutes left. I don't get it – I'm typing as fast as I can but I've hardly got anywhere! So anyway, my mum went off to work just as Tone-Deaf got back. I hate it when I hear his rattly cab pulling up outside, my stomach always does this weird thing where it feels like it's being flipped over like a pancake and my mouth goes as dry as sandpaper. When he came in this morning he did what he always does, he gave Michaela a massive hug and said, 'Hello, Princess,' and kissed her on top of her head but he just nodded to me and said, 'Get us a cup of tea,' even though I've been nice to him all week and trying to understand why he is the way he is, like you told me to. So I got him some tea and also some toast without even being asked and as soon as he went to his bedroom I called upstairs to ask if I could take Michaela to Jessica's for the day. My heart beat so fast while I waited for his answer I seriously thought it might burst. And when he did finally say, 'Yeah, OK,' I nearly died of shock. I couldn't believe how easy it had been! I didn't relax though until I got to the community centre. I kept thinking, what if it's a trap and Tone-Deaf has followed us? Or what if they won't let Michaela stay? Or what if Michaela tells on me? But, underneath it all, part of me didn't really care any more. I'm so tired of feeling sad. And waiting for other people to make me happy and they don't. And if no one else is going to make you happy, well maybe you just have to do it for yourself.

And I'm SO glad I went because it was SO frost-free! The drama teacher's name is Debbie and she has really lovely hair and – oh no – why is time going so quickly? Look, I'm going to take Michaela home now and get the vegetables done and then I'll try and pop back later so I can tell you about the rest of my exciting day. I can't believe what a multi-coloured, frost-free day it's been. And tomorrow we have the auditions! More later, I hope – the library is open till 8 tonight so it should be OK.

Your e-mate and fellow actress (well, sort of anyway),
Georgie xx

....

From: nancyblue#@aol.com
To: georgie*harris@hotmail.com
Date: Mon, 31 July 17:10
Subject: Re: OMG!

Dear Georgie,

Oh my goodness – how exciting! And how could you leave me hanging like that without even telling me what happened at the workshop?! You really are a born storyteller, darling, talk about building dramatic tension. But to leave before you even get to the denouement – well, that's just cruel ;)

Incidentally, what does that ;) symbol mean? Dylan does them a lot in his emails to me and I'm too embarrassed to ask!

Your email reminded me a bit of that quiz show Who Wants to Be a Millionaire? when a contestant has made it all the way to the final question only for that smug host to give a lop-sided smirk to the camera and say, 'Will Mr Bloggs from Bognor Regis make it to one million pounds and change his life forever more? You'll have to wait until next week because we're out of time!'

There's so much I want to say in response to what you did write, but I guess I'll wait and see if I hear from you again today.

Yours dying from the suspense,
Nan xx

....

From: georgie*harris@hotmail.com
To: nancyblue#@aol.com
Date: Mon, 31 July 18:13
Subject: Best Day Ever – Part Two

Dear Nan,

I'm so sorry – no matter how hard I try I seem to end up rambling on about other stuff and never get to the point. So this time I am determined to tell you exactly what happened at the workshop. As you can see, I managed to get back to the library and I have a whole 45 minutes before I have to be home and it only takes about 5 minutes to get home so I have a whole 40 minutes to write to you! I really feel as if the heavens are smiling on me today – everything is going so well for once. What does that actually mean by the way

– the heavens are smiling on me? I heard a supermodel say it on Oprah the other day when she was talking about how her whole life has been transformed since she gave up eating wheat. Is it another way of saying that God must be happy with me and making nice things happen? Or does it mean that the people in heaven are actually smiling at me? I hope it's the second one because then it could mean that my dad is smiling down on me and making nice stuff happen. And maybe your husband Bruce is with him too? Maybe they both know we're emailing each other so they've made friends too? Oh God, I've just realised I'm rambling again aren't I? Sorry!!!! What does denouement mean? Sorry, I just thought that while I was on the subject of things I don't understand . . . And where is your computer? I'd like to be able to picture you as you write to me.

OK – the drama workshop. It's being held in the community centre at the bottom of the high street, about 15 minutes from here. Actually it doesn't look like a community centre at all – it looks like a really old barn. But that's because it IS a really old barn! The oldest surviving barn in London apparently. Only it isn't used as a barn any more because the council bought it and all the other old farm buildings, and converted them into halls and offices and stuff. But it still looks dead nice, with oak beams in the ceilings and a duck pond in the courtyard and this really quaint tea room called the Cow Pat or the Cow Byre or something, next to what used to be the old farmhouse.

So anyway, the drama workshop is in the barn on the left of the duck pond. (If you're facing it from the road. If you're facing it from the car park it's on the right.) I was dead nervous when I first got there, what with being scared Tone-Deaf had followed us and everything. And it was even worse when I actually walked into the barn because all the other kids were there already and of course none of them had a little sister with them so they were all staring at me and it was really embarrassing and I could feel my cheeks just burning and burning. But then Debbie the workshop leader came over and she was really smiley and friendly, not like the teachers at Ruislip Gardens High at all, and she asked me my name. And then Jessica came over and she said in a really loud voice, pointing to Michaela, 'George, why have you brought her, you know it's only for twelve to sixteen year olds?' I couldn't even look at Debbie I was so embarrassed. I just stared at the floor and muttered, 'My name's Georgie,' but I said the '-ie' part really loud. Then thankfully Debbie got all the other kids to do some warm-up stretches before she came back over to me. I explained to her that I had to look after Michaela because my mum was working but she was a really good kid and wouldn't be any trouble and I had brought loads of toys for her to play with.

Debbie just sort of stood there for a moment, frowning and thinking about it and then Michaela said, 'You look just like a princess.' And then Debbie started to laugh and said, 'Oh well, I don't see why not.' Sometimes I really love Michaela!!

So, once Debbie had taken my name and age and what school I go to and all that stuff, we made a little play area for Michaela down by the front of the stage and then we did a load of drama exercises. I never realised acting could be so much fun! First we did this game where we all had to walk around the hall and Debbie would call out, 'Let's all be . . .' and then she'd say different things like 'an elephant' or 'a tree' or 'a ballerina', and we had to walk around pretending to be it. (Michaela REALLY liked that game!) Then Debbie let us call out the instructions. I said, 'Let's all be people who've just found out we've won the lottery.' (I pretend that one a lot when I'm at home lol!) Jessica said, 'Let's all be supermodels' – the boys hated that one. Then this really rough-looking boy called Dread – only he spells it Dred and I'm sure it's not his real name – said, 'Let's all be drunk.' All the other kids thought that was hilarious but I didn't. I don't like drunk people, I think they're sad, not funny. But obviously I didn't say anything and anyway, straight after that, Debbie made us do a different exercise. This time we had to get into pairs and one of us had to pretend to be the other one's reflection in a mirror. I had to be Jessica's reflection, and it was really hard work because she was being well moody. 'Why did you have to bring Michaela,' she hissed at me, while miming brushing her hair. I mimed brushing my own hair back (although it isn't nearly as long, blonde or pretty as hers). 'I couldn't help it,' I hissed. 'My mum and Tony are working.' Jessica gave a long sigh and shook her head. Then she said, 'Why are you looking so miserable?' I didn't have the heart to tell her I was trying to be her reflection! But then, when we were all called over to sit in a circle, I realised why she was in such a strop. Jamie Phelps hadn't turned up. I think the only reason Jessica came to the workshop was because she was hoping he would be there. Even though she says if she can't be a supermodel she's going to be an actress. Next, Debbie gave us a talk about drama and how she wanted us all to have a lot of fun for the next three weeks and how much we were going to enjoy Bugsy Malone and that we'd have to work hard but it would all be worth it on the final night when we put the show on for our parents. I'm trying not to think about that bit. How could I invite my mum and Tone-Deaf to the show after they both said I couldn't come to the workshop?!

The next thing we had to do was take it in turns to act out different emotions and the others had to guess what we were supposed to be feeling. I pretended to be excited, which didn't really work because most people shouted out 'shocked' and Dred shouted out 'having a fit' — stupid skanksta. (That's my name for boys like him by the way — boys who think they're really hard and dress like gangstas but really just look skanky with their pants on display for the whole world to see.) Everyone got Jessica when she did bored because she was so realistic! But then, just before lunch, Jamie Phelps finally turned up and Jessica was like a different person. It's funny how some people are like human E numbers, isn't it? When Jamie walked in it was like the whole room lit up and everyone seemed to get a whole lot more lively. Not just Jessica and the other girls, but most of the boys too. It's not like he even did anything either. I think it's just the way he is. He has all this thick dark hair brushed forward over his cheekbones and these big dark-brown eyes that always seem to be dreaming of something else, something far better. And he walks in a different way to everyone else too, all slowly like he's got all the time in the world, with his hands in his pockets and his head sort of tilted to one side. Maybe that's why everyone loves him so much, because they want to know what his secret is and wish they could be a part of it. Even Debbie seemed to get all giggly and bouncy after he arrived, and she didn't even get cross that he was an hour and a half late!

At lunchtime the other kids were allowed to go and hang

out on the grass by the duck pond but Debbie said Michaela and I had to stay in the hall because Michaela was too young. I didn't really mind though, I was just so glad to be there. Then in the afternoon Debbie got us to take it in turns to sing a song of our choice. Jessica was great of course. She has singing classes every Thursday night because if she doesn't make it as a supermodel or an actress she's going to be a pop star. And Jamie was fantastic, he has a proper rock-star voice and he sang this song that he'd written himself about being trapped in a prison, where 'the air is cold as ice and fear grips his heart like a vice, vice, vice'. Jessica says he's already in a band with some of his mates and he's the lead singer and guitarist. I bet Debbie casts them in the main roles, they were definitely the best singers by far. Jessica says if she gets to be Blousey and Jamie is Bugsy she will never ask God for another thing in her whole entire life.

I was the last one to get to sing and I was kind of hoping I wouldn't have to because it was getting really near to going-home time. A lot of the other kids were getting bored so it was a bit off-putting because they were chatting and messing about and when I first tried to sing, my voice came out like a little squeak. Then Debbie shouted at Dred and his friends to stop mucking around and for everyone to be quiet and show me some respect. But that only made it worse because then I was standing there all alone on the stage with everyone staring at me in total silence and it was SO embarrassing. I really got the urge to giggle too – not because it was funny, because it wasn't AT ALL – but because I really didn't want to do it. And the worst thing was, the song I'd chosen to do was Wonderful Tonight, the one my dad sang to my mum the night they met, and it's a really slow love song and not funny at all. So I did what I always do when I'm trying not to laugh, I thought of my dad. But this time instead of seeing him lying on the road and dying and stuff I saw him standing behind the curtain at the side of the stage and he was smiling one of his lovely smiles at me. Then I saw his lips move and I'm sure I could hear him whispering, 'Go on, Georgie, you can do it.' So I closed my eyes and sang as if I was singing just to him.

I didn't open my eyes again till I'd got to the end of the song and when I did everyone was still sitting there in total silence and Debbie was sniffing and wiping her eyes. So I said, 'Er, I've finished,' and she said, 'Yes, I know, thank you, that was lovely,' and then everyone started to clap really loudly and someone (I think it was Jamie) did this really loud whistle and cheer!!! Oh Nan, it was so amazing. Afterwards loads of the others came over and said well done and even Dred the skanksta nodded his head at me as we were leaving. Was it like that for you when you acted on stage? I googled you again (so make sure you tell your friend Ricardo!) and I saw you won an award when you played Lady Macbeth, so you must have had tons of applause. It makes you feel so amazing, doesn't it? Like you could be or do anything.

I hope your meal went OK on Sunday. Maybe you could suggest doing something different with your friends next time? Something that you never did with your husband, like bowling or going to the cinema. It might not hurt so much.

Oh no – time's almost up on the computer. Will let you know tomorrow how the auditions went. Hope I don't get the giggles or squeak again ;) (That symbol is meant to be a smiley face and a wink by the way – you get neck ache trying to see it though!!)

Lots of love, your e-mate,
Georgie xxx

PS: Would it be all right for me to use vegetable oil on my hair? We don't have any olive oil. When I asked Tone-Deaf if we could get some he said olive oil was for greasy spicks – whatever that means!

From: nancyblue#@aol.com
To: georgie*harris@hotmail.com
Date: Mon, 31 July 18:42
Subject: Re: Best Day Ever – Part Two

Dear Georgie,

I was online checking out botox injections (it really comes to something when you're considering paralysing your forehead in order to look more youthful!) when your message just pinged into my inbox. How wonderfully exciting!! The heavens really do seem to be smiling upon you and I'm so pleased, darling, because it's no more than you deserve. And what a lovely idea thinking of your dad and Bruce up there together smiling down on both of us. It's what I'm going to choose to believe too, I think they'd get on famously.
;) ;)
– that's Bruce and your dad winking and grinning at us!

So, your singing moved your teacher to tears? Something tells me you may be cast as more than a chorus member or an undertaker this time, darling. Oh, it's all so exciting and I cannot wait to hear how you get on. I'm replying as fast as I can just in case you're still online because I wanted to give you some advice. As someone who has been to more than her fair share of auditions, a top tip is to get 'into the zone' beforehand. This is similar to what athletes do when preparing for an event – they become fully focused on winning and don't think about a single other thing. When acting you must literally become the part you are playing. As soon as you get given your part to read for the audition, become her. Think of the mannerisms and body language she'd use. Think of HOW she'd talk, not just what she's saying. And above all – do what you did today, block everyone else out and enjoy. Good luck, Georgie, darling. I'm going to send this right now so there's a chance you get it before leaving the library.

Lots of love,
Nan xx

PS: Not sure if vegetable oil is quite as effective as olive oil but you could give it a go!
PPS: 'Denouement' means the exciting climax of a story.
PPS: My computer is in Bruce's study – an attic room with sloping ceilings overlooking the sea. It is so unbelievably peaceful up here. Sometimes when I have the windows flung open it feels as if I am sitting on a cloud, especially when a seagull swoops by, calling for his friends!

From: georgie*harris@hotmail.com

To: nancyblue#@aol.com

Date: Mon, 31 July 18:46

Subject: Re: Best Day Ever – Part Two

Thank you!!!!

Gx

....

From: nancyblue#@aol.com

To: georgie*harris@hotmail.com

Date: Tue, 1 August 07:03

Subject: Good Morning

Dear Georgie,

Oh dear – I'm afraid I must be one of the most impatient people in the entire world and waiting to hear how you've got on at your audition is absolutely killing me!! To make matters worse it's only 7 o'clock in the morning so you haven't even been to the workshop yet, but I couldn't sleep and it's such a glorious morning I got up an hour ago and took Woodstock down to the beach to watch the sun rise over the sea.

I find it very hard to sleep these days to be truthful. The bed seems as vast as a desert without Bruce and so bloody empty, no matter how many cushions I curl up against. I have absolutely nothing against girls swearing by the way – if we didn't swear we'd be driven to murder I'm certain! So anyway, I seem to spend most of my time nowadays wishing I was in bed when I'm up and then wishing I was up when I'm in bed. Being up and about is getting a little easier actually. I find I have good days and bad days. Of course at first it was all bad days – in fact it didn't feel like days at all, just one long black tunnel of shock and despair. Bruce's death was so sudden you see. Not as sudden as your dad's, but his cancer wasn't the type to linger – ironic really as Bruce was a real live wire too. Perhaps illnesses are like dogs and they find matching owners? Woodstock is certainly like me – quite the drama queen and loves an audience. Anyway in typical hyperactive fashion, within a month of being diagnosed, Bruce was dead, so at first I was still dealing with the shock of him being seriously ill, let alone gone. But recently I've begun getting the odd good day here and there. Of course they're never as good as when he was here, but at least I can make it through without crying too much, and sometimes I even feel quite glad to be here.

I think today is going to be one of the better ones. The sun looked so beautiful shimmering down on the sea, causing it to gleam like a sheet of gold, and the pebbles on the beach glistening like banks of amber beside it. I just stood there and drank it all in and I was so thankful to witness such beauty, even though Bruce wasn't there to see it with me.

I hope it is sunny where you are. And I hope you wake up with sunny thoughts too. I think I might even get my watercolours out later and do a bit of painting in the garden – anything to while away the time until I hear your news! I might bake a cake too. Dylan and Bruce always loved my cakes, especially my millionaire's shortbread. It's funny really, when you live on your own you stop doing nice things because it doesn't seem worth it. But why ever not? What a sorry state of affairs it is when you don't think it's worth treating yourself. Do you know what? I'm even going to go and buy myself some flowers! Will be thinking of you, darling, and sending you lots of good-luck vibes.

Lots of love,
Nan xx

....

From: georgie*harris@hotmail.com
To: nancyblue#@aol.com
Date: Tue, 1 August 17:11
Subject: Hip Hip Hip Hooray

Oh Nan, I am so excited I can hardly speak, or write, or do anything at all except hug myself and keep wondering if this is all a dream and any moment now I'll wake up and Tone-Deaf will be scratching his hairy belly and telling me to make him something and all I'll have to look forward to is a day of chores and being shouted at. I'm a bit scared too. And a little worried. OK – a lot worried. Sorry it's taken me so long to email you but I had to go straight home after the workshop this afternoon because Tone-Deaf wanted to take Michaela over to his mum's for tea. Today I told him we were going to the cinema with Jessica and her parents so we wouldn't be back earlier than 4.15. I was terrified he was going to say no, but then Michaela kept begging him to let us go so he had to give in. I bought Michaela two packs of Jelly Babies on the way to the workshop to say thank you!

After a few warm-up exercises Debbie split us into groups of four. Jessica, me, Dred and Jamie were all in the same group and we had to take it in turns to read the parts of Blousey and Bugsy in the scene where they first meet.

Jessica and Jamie were great, but when me and Dred had to do it he kept putting me off by reading his lines in a really stupid gangster voice. I know it is a play about gangsters but it's set in America not London and he kept adding 'd'ya know what I mean' and 'innit' on the end of all his lines. I tried to get into the zone like you said but it was really distracting when he wasn't even saying what he was supposed to and then, when we got to the end of the scene where he says 'pleased to meet you' and is meant to shake my hand, he tried to high-five me and then he shouted 'respect, man' so loud I jumped out of my skin. After that Debbie got us to swap partners and Jamie Phelps and I had to play Bugsy and Tallulah in the scene where she kisses him on the forehead! I couldn't believe it – and in front of Jessica as well! At first I was dead embarrassed but then I finally managed to do what you said and got into the zone and didn't look at Jessica AT ALL. Jamie made it easier because he said all of his lines properly and was actually really good for someone who goes around looking like he doesn't really care about anything at all! I felt terrible afterwards though, especially when Jessica had to kiss that horrible skanksta, Dred. She looked furious and gave him more of a head-butt than a kiss. After the auditions we had our lunch break. Jessica went storming straight out to the duck pond with the two Kates and I couldn't go after her to say sorry because I had to stay inside with Michaela.

Michaela wanted to have a turn up on the stage so I let her have a pretend audition and got her to sing her favourite Tigger song from Winnie-the-Pooh. Just as she finished this voice from behind me said, 'So singing runs in the family then?' And when I turned round Jamie Phelps was standing down by the front of the stage, sort of half smiling through his long fringe. Straight away my cheeks began to burn. I really hate my face when it does that; it's as if part of my own body has rebelled against me and likes to shame me at the most embarrassing moments possible! I tried to cover it up by turning away, which must have looked dead rude, but I didn't want him thinking I liked him or anything, because I don't, obviously, but my cheeks seem to have an evil twisted mind all of their own. Then I heard this clambering sound and when I turned round Jamie had got up on the stage behind me. And then he asked Michaela if she could do the Tigger dance and the next thing I know the pair of them are bouncing round the stage shouting 'hee hee hee hee!' And then, as they bounced past me Jamie grabbed my hand and said, 'Come on – join in.' So then the three of us were bouncing around like mad and it was so strange because I would never in a million years have thought that someone as cool as Jamie would even know who Tigger was, let alone want to play being him! Even when Michaela pretended to be a heffalump (they are the monsters in Winnie-the-Pooh) and tried to eat him alive he didn't mind, he just looked at me and laughed and then pretended to be dead. He really is a good actor, but not as good as Dylan of course! Then Michaela pretended to bite me so I lay down next to Jamie and pretended to be dead as well, and when I peeped out of the corner of my eye he was looking at me and smiling. But it was a nice smile, not the piss-taking kind that boys usually do. (I'm so glad you don't mind girls swearing!) Then, just as I started to smile back and pray that my cheeks would not combust, I heard someone coughing loudly behind me and Jessica saying, 'George, what the hell are you doing?' Jamie sprang straight up, ruffled Michaela's hair and said in this really gruff voice, 'I'm going outside.' I got up really quickly too and started to explain the game to Jessica but she'd already turned around and followed Jamie out of the barn. After that Michaela and I just sat quietly on the edge of the stage and I told her a story about a princess who was allergic to kisses so she was really sad because she couldn't marry her prince. But all the time I couldn't stop thinking about Jamie and Jessica and what had just happened. And then Michaela said, 'Is Jamie your prince?' and I said, 'What are you talking about? Of course he isn't.' And she said, 'Well why did you kiss him earlier then?' Kids, eh!!

After lunch I thought Jessica was going to be all grumpy with me again but she was fine. She came straight over and sat with me and I could smell cigarettes mingled in with her perfume. She kept smiling this private little smile too, as if she knew this really cool secret. Maybe Jamie gave her a cigarette and maybe something else happened, I don't know. But what I do know is this – I'VE GOT ONE OF THE MAIN PARTS!!!!

Can you believe it? Debbie read the cast list out after lunch and she started off with all the small parts like the undertakers and the girl singers and every time I waited for my name to be called out but it didn't come. Then she got on to the bigger parts and there was still no mention of me. At that point I seriously thought she had forgotten all about me and then I thought maybe she was going to ask me to leave after today because I wasn't allowed to bring Michaela any more. I started to feel really sick at that thought, especially when Jessica got the part of Tallulah. But then things all got really weird because Dred was cast as Fat Sam – and after he messed about in his audition too!! And Debbie said really quickly, 'Blousey – Georgie Harris, and Bugsy – Jamie Phelps.' I was in total shock. She picked me for Blousey!!! One of the majorest roles in the whole thing. And the same part you played too! How frost-free is that? When I looked up the first person I saw was Jamie and he was smiling that really nice half smile at me again. I was a little bit worried about how Jessica would take it because I know she really wanted to be Blousey, but she was OK. Perhaps Jamie finally asked her out at lunchtime? On the way home she said she was 'super pleased' she got Tallulah because it was the best role to showcase both her singing and acting talents as she has a bigger solo than Blousey. I don't care though, I prefer Blousey's song, even if it is shorter. It's so full of meaning and emotion, and trust me, I know all about being an 'ordinary fool'! And I'm just so pleased to have a big part for once. And scared. But I'm trying not to think of the actual performance just yet. There isn't any point worrying about it, is there? Somehow or other I'll get to do it. And get Michaela to keep quiet. And remember all my lines. Oh God, there's so much to worry about! But not today. Today I am going to celebrate.

It's been really sunny here too and it's funny because on my way to the library I was looking at all the trees around the edge of the park and how the sun was coming through them in thin rays of gold as if it was being sieved through the gaps in the leaves. It was dead pretty and I felt so happy – just like you did this morning. I was sorry to hear that you can't sleep though. Do you know what I do when I can't sleep? I talk to my dad. Not out loud because I might wake Michaela up, but in my head. I close my eyes really tight and I imagine he's sitting next to me in the dark. And then I tell him all the stuff that's on my mind. And the best thing is, usually I can hear what he'd say too, if I concentrate hard enough.

You should try it with your husband. When you cuddle up next to your cushions, you should imagine that they're him and then tell him all the stuff that's bothering you and see what happens. See if you can hear him reply.

I hope you did buy yourself some flowers. I love flowers. They always make me feel all bright and sunny inside, especially daisies. When I was little, Angelica would make me daisy chains every time we went to the park. She'd make one to go on my head like a crown and then one for my neck and a smaller one for my wrist. I used to wish I was called Daisy when I was little too. It's such a pretty name – not like Georgie. I even wrote inside the cover of all of my books, 'This book belongs to Daisy Harris'. I don't mind being called Georgie so much now though, as long as certain people don't call me George!

I've just had an idea. I'm going to go to the park and make my mum a daisy chain for when she gets home from work and then I'm going to put it on her head and crown her Princess Angelica and tell her that I'm going to wait on her hand and foot because she is a beautiful princess and isn't allowed to do any work. I won't call her a parasite though!! Lol!

Hope you've had a lovely day and thanks so much for your

frost-free advice about the audition — it really paid off. If you have any advice about playing Blousey I would be really grateful. I'll email you tomorrow with the latest from the rehearsals. How is Dylan getting on with his film in America? I bet you must be missing him.

Love from your e-mate,
Georgie xx

....

From: nancyblue#@aol.com
To: georgie*harris@hotmail.com
Date: Tue, 1 August 23.48
Subject: Hurrah!!!

Dearest Georgie,

Oh my goodness — I fell asleep during a particularly boring episode of Murder She Wrote. (When are they ever going to realise that it has to be the daft old bag herself committing all the murders? Everywhere she goes she leaves a trail of corpses!) Now it is a quarter to midnight and I have only just read your email and your splendid news. YOU GOT BLOUSEY!!! I am so proud of you, darling, and so excited.

I had a feeling something like this would happen when you wrote about your teacher's reaction to your song the day before. OK, now I need to compose myself and write you some really 'frost-free' advice. Blousey is a wonderful role to be given and you are exactly right – her song, Ordinary Fool, is beautiful and so full of poignancy.

Usually the first thing an actor does on being given a part is to go through the script and highlight all of their lines. Then you go through again looking for the true motivation behind each line. For instance, on the surface a line might seem to be happy and jolly but if you know that your character is feeling a little blue at that point in the play then you have to show that somehow, either through the delivery of the line or something in the character's body language. Make little notes in the margins of your script if you can, to help you remember how to play each line. Also think about how your character feels about each of the other characters and again make sure you reflect that somehow in your acting. For example, the way Blousey really feels about Bugsy even when she is being mad at him. How can you let the audience see that she loves him underneath? I must say your leading man, Jamie, sounds rather intriguing. I am SO glad you weren't cast alongside the dreadful-sounding Dred! Oh Georgie, I am so, so happy for you. You see – if you want something badly enough it really CAN come true.

Today has been quite magical, hasn't it? It was as if the sunshine first thing cast a spell on both of us, making everything go right. You got your part and I actually went a whole day without shedding a tear. I walked Woodstock, I painted, I made a lemon drizzle cake and I bought some yellow roses just for me. And I felt a contentment I haven't felt in months. Perhaps the sun's rays were the warmth of Bruce and your father's smiles beaming down on us? I am going to go to bed now and I'm going to try what you suggested. I'm going to talk to Bruce as if he were still here with me. And do you know what? Instead of wailing 'why?' like I usually do, I'm just going to tell him how much I love him.

Goodnight, Georgie, and please let me know how you get on in your first rehearsal.

Lots of love,
Nan xx

PS: Dylan is getting on fabulously across the pond – apart from a small accident when they were filming with some remote-controlled jellyfish and he got a slight electric shock. I know – don't ask!

From: georgie*harris@hotmail.com
To: nancyblue#@aol.com
Date: Wed, 2 August 17:29
Subject: Disaster!!!

Dear Nan,

Disaster has struck! I am writing to you from the library (surprise, surprise!) with an oil slick on my head and the weight of an entire day's humiliation pressing down upon my shoulders. The older I get the more it feels like a curse to have been born a woman. Not only do we get stupid periods every month and have to hobble around bent over in agony, but we also have the terrible responsibility of looking effortlessly beautiful all of the time. I tried your tip for shiny hair last night – using some vegetable oil that I snuck from the kitchen when no one was looking. Tone-Deaf cooks just about everything he eats in oil so I didn't want him to catch me using it! I did as you said and used about half a cupful on my hair and combed it right through before going to bed. In the morning I looked just like Michelle Price (this girl at school who no one talks to because she talks like a dalek and smells of wee. She also never seems to wash her hair and it is so greasy it clings together in dark clumps and you can see her scalp shining through as white as snow). This morning when I went into the bathroom and looked in the mirror that is exactly how I looked. But I wasn't worried because I knew when I washed the oil off I would have the shiniest hair in all of Ruislip.

Oh Nan, if only that were true. The sad fact is I ended up keeping the greasiest hair in all of Ruislip (and that includes Michelle Price) because our water wasn't working! A mains in our road had burst during the night and the council had to cut off the supply to the whole street. Of course I didn't know all that at first. All I knew was when I got into the shower and turned it on nothing happened. I thought it was just the shower that was broken so I went over to the sink, thinking I could rinse my hair with the jug, the way mum washes Michaela's hair, but no. I turned on the hot and then the cold tap and still nothing came out. Have you ever had a moment of complete and utter panic, where you just want to die or find an underground cave in a deep dark forest where you can hide away forever? Well this was one of those moments. I stood there gaping into the mirror at my pale, shell-shocked face surrounded by dark, greasy clumps of hair, and random words kept echoing around my head, as if the King of Embarrassment himself was standing in there shouting into a megaphone: JUST LIKE MICHELLE PRICE! REHEARSALS! JESSICA AND THE TWO KATES! ALL THE OTHER KIDS! JAMIE PHELPS! DRED! DEBBIE! SHAME! DIE! OH! MY! GOD!

I somehow managed to stay out of Angelica's way while she got ready for work, ransacking my room for something to put on my head to hide my vile hair. In the end all I could find was a tatty old pink cap I've had since I was seven with a picture of the Carebears on the front. Can you imagine how skanky it was? But what else could I do? Faced with the choice of looking like an immature, Carebear-loving kid or a greasy old fleabag I had no option. Of course Michaela thought the cap was great and starting whinging about how she wanted to wear it, so I had to blackmail her with the promise of even more Jelly Babies. Then, just after mum had left for work and I'd finally plucked up the courage to set foot outside the house, Tone-Deaf pulled up in his cab with a face like thunder. Why do people say that? 'A face like thunder.' For a start you can't see thunder so how can a face look like it? And also, thunder is a noise but if someone has a face like thunder it isn't roaring or growling is it? It just looks really mean. And Tone-Deaf did look really mean. One of the back windows on his cab was smashed and when he got out I saw that the knuckles on his right hand were all grazed and bleeding.

As soon as he spotted us coming out of the front door he told us to get back in the house because he wanted some breakfast. And of course he couldn't want toast or something simple, he had to want a big fry-up. And let me tell you the

LAST thing I wanted to see this morning was any more vegetable oil!! But of course I had no choice. I knew I had to do whatever he wanted if I was going to be allowed to go out. While I started cooking he went up to the bathroom and a few minutes later I heard all this shouting and a massive crash. I actually dropped the bacon on the floor, it gave me such a fright. I thought he must have found a burglar or something. I turned off the cooker and put Michaela into the front porch so she could get away quickly if she needed to. Then I crept upstairs as quietly as a mouse so I could find out what was going on without being spotted and be able to call the police if I needed to. But there wasn't an intruder at all. When I got to the bathroom I peeped through the crack in the door and saw Tone-Deaf leaning over the sink saying all these really rude words, which I won't repeat here because they were too rude, even for women who agree that swearing is sometimes essential. Then I peered around the door to the other side of the bathroom and I saw bits of glass all over the floor. I must have gasped out loud, because the next thing I knew Tone Deaf had come flying out of the bathroom all red in the face, with the vein on the side of his forehead that always comes out when he's stressed bulging away like a frog's throat.

'How long have you been there?' he yelled at me and then he called me a 'nosy little brat', which was like, totally wrong on so many levels (as Jessica would have said). Firstly, I wasn't being nosy, I was being concerned. Secondly, I'm not little, I'm fourteen years old and in certain countries like Africa and stuff I would be married with three kids by now – although I'm really glad I'm not! And thirdly, I'm not a brat. A brat always demands her own way and I never do. I always put up with everything just to keep the peace. If I was a brat I would have demanded that I go to the drama workshop, not stay at home to make his stupid breakfast. So I just put my head down and said, 'I only just got here. I came to check you were OK.' See, I was still trying to be nice to him. But of course it didn't make any difference. 'Oh you were, were you?' he replied. 'Well, would you mind telling me why there's no f***ing water?'

At first I couldn't believe it. Was that what he was so mad about? Had he really trashed the bathroom just because there was no water? I peeked around him into the room to check I hadn't been seeing things, but the glass was still there on the floor. I wish I hadn't though because the next thing I knew he'd pulled me into the bathroom and now his hand was bleeding really badly and he said, 'You want a good look? Well, why don't you clean it all up?' Once I was in there I could see where all the glass had come from – he'd smashed the shower door. I felt a bit sick then, but I didn't want to say anything or even look at him so I started picking up the bits of broken glass and putting them on top of the washing basket. And all the time I knew he was still standing there because I could hear him breathing all funny like he'd just run a race or something. Then I heard a wailing sound coming from downstairs and I remembered Michaela out in the porch. But it was OK because Tone-Deaf heard her too and he went straight downstairs. I was really scared he might get mad at her for making a noise but he didn't. I crept out on to the landing and I heard him talking to her in the nice gentle voice that he keeps especially for her, telling her that there'd been this really big spider in the bathroom and it was poisonous and he was worried it might attack us so he had to kill it.

Isn't it funny how with just the right words you can completely change the truth of a thing? In that couple of sentences Tone-Deaf went from being a mad psycho shower-attacker to a heroic child-saver. He was so convincing that if I hadn't seen the bathroom with my very own eyes I would have believed him too. It isn't just that he has a different voice for Michaela — he's a whole different person for her. A hero rather than a bully.

After I'd cleared up the glass I really didn't want to go downstairs. I really didn't want to do anything, my hands were all trembly and my eyes were all watery. But it was getting later and later and I had to get to the drama workshop, so I brought the glass down into the kitchen in an old plastic bag. Tone-Deaf was sitting at the table with a tea towel wrapped around his bleeding hand and Michaela on his knee. They were singing Incey Wincey Spider. I walked straight past them and put the glass in the bin. Then I went over to the cooker and turned the hob back on. 'It's all right,' Tone Deaf said from behind me. 'I'll do that. You take your sister out for a bit.' And when I turned round he was holding out a £20 note. 'Take her to the flicks or something,' he said, and for once he was using his gentle Michaela voice on me. It all felt a bit like a dream so I took the money from him as quickly as possible in case I woke up.

We had to run all the way to the workshop and even then we were fifteen minutes late. Luckily Debbie was OK about it, but I could see Jessica frowning at me and shaking her head. Then she whispered something to the two Kates and they all started to giggle. With all the drama at home I'd forgotten about the stupid Carebears cap, but despite the embarrassment I knew it was still a lot better than the greasy hair underneath, so I ignored them and turned away.

The first thing we did today was sit in a circle and do a read-through. Debbie said this is what all professional actors do before they begin rehearsals so I suppose you know all about them? Do you find that when something horrible happens the moment you wake up, the rest of the day all goes wrong too? That is what today has been like for me. First no water and greasy hair. Then Tone-Deaf going mental. Then having to turn up to rehearsals in a Carebear cap. And then I totally messed up my read through. First of all I read my first line all wrong, telling Jamie to 'lip the zip' instead of 'zip the lip'! And then of course my cheeks began to burn and I think the heat must have melted my eyes or something because the words on my script all started swimming about like fishes. Jessica was sitting across from me and I could hear her sighing every time I got something wrong, which made it even worse.

As soon as Debbie gave us a break I rushed out to the toilets. I don't know how I stopped myself from crying – I think it was the thought of having red eyes as well as greasy hair and a stupid cap. When I finally pulled myself together and came out of the toilets, Jamie Phelps was sitting on the window ledge in the corridor staring outside. I was so ashamed I tried to shuffle straight past him and back into the hall, but just as I drew level with him he said, 'Look.' I stopped dead in my tracks and said, 'What?' 'Look,' he said again, still not turning round but nodding towards the sky. I followed his gaze way up to where a cloud was drifting by, its edges all pinky gold from the sun. 'Makes you think, doesn't it?' he said. I nodded, although I wasn't really sure what he meant. Then Debbie called that break was over so we had to go back in.

After that things got a little better. We had got to Act Two in the read-through and as Jessica sang her opening song (really well of course, with her long blonde hair all shiny and grease-free) I thought about what Jamie had said about the cloud and I tried to figure out what it had made him think. That we should pretend to be just like clouds and drift through life without a care in the world, even when our hair looks like an oil slick and our mum is married to a psycho? That the universe is so ginormous our lives and our problems don't really mean all that much at all? That clouds can be lots of different colours, not just grey and white? I couldn't decide, and I wished I'd had the courage to ask him. But then it was our scene and when it got to the bit where Bugsy kisses his finger and touches Blousey on the nose I couldn't help looking over my script at Jamie and he was looking straight back at me and smiling that lazy smile of his again. And then I knew for sure what he meant when he said 'it makes you think' because I felt a tingling right down in the pit of my stomach. And I realised that no matter how bad things get, there is always a silver (or in this case, pinky gold) lining. Seeing a beautiful sky or smile, or hearing a beautiful song, can make you feel more alive than you ever thought possible.

Unfortunately at lunchtime things all went wrong again. Jessica and the two Kates came straight over to see me as soon as the read-through finished and Jessica started interrogating me about the cap. In the end I had to explain what had happened and took it off and showed them my hair. I had hoped that Jessica would understand after her recent disaster with the pink hair dye, but she just shook her head really slowly and gave this massive sigh as if to say, 'Oh George, you are like, so totally naff.' I was actually quite relieved when they all went outside and left me alone with Michaela.

Thankfully we finished a bit early this afternoon because Debbie had a doctor's appointment. I didn't even bother waiting to walk with Jessica and the two Kates I felt so tired and fed up. Isn't it funny how two days right next to each other can be so different? Yesterday I was so full of energy I felt like Michaela's clockwork mouse when it has been wound up as far as it will go and shoots around all over the place. But today I just wanted to crawl back home with my Carebear-capped head slumped in misery. To make matters worse Michaela was being really grumpy because she'd got dead bored having to stay quiet while we'd been reading for hours. I had to spend most of Tone-Deaf's twenty pounds on presents for her to make up for it, even though I was dying to buy myself a decent cap. Then I had to persuade her to lie and say we'd been to Jessica's to watch High School Musical again. 'Don't want to!' she kept shouting all the way back through the park. It was only when I started to cry that she finally stopped. I don't usually cry, honest, but it had been such a rubbish day and I was so scared she would tell Tone-Deaf about the drama workshop and I would be grounded for about a million years, I couldn't help it. I'm kind of glad I did though because it made Michaela go back to being her cute self again. She gave me a massive cuddle and wiped my tears away with her tiny fingers and said, 'Don't worry Georgie, I still love you. I will come to the workshop (only she pronounces it 'wordshop') tomorrow (only she pronounces it 'tomowow') as long as you buy me three packs of Jelly Babies.'

By the time we got back to our road I was really nervous again. We live in a cul-de-sac (a dead-end street – just like my life, ha, ha!) shaped like a lollipop. You walk up a long straight bit (like the lolly stick) and then the road goes round in a circle, with a green and some trees in the middle, and eventually comes back to the stick bit again. Our house is at the top part of the circle, so you can't see it properly till you get halfway round the green. Nothing ever happens in our road. If boredom had a capital city then all its streets would be as dreary as Dulverton Close. But today, with every step I took, I felt a little bit sicker. What if Tone-Deaf had gone back into a rage after we'd left and smashed up the rest of the house? What if he'd burnt it to the ground because he couldn't have a shower? But when we came round the bend I saw his mate Darren's van parked in the driveway with the remains of the old shower door on the back of it. While we'd been out, Darren had come and fitted a whole new shower unit. Tone-Deaf had had his cab window fixed too. It was as if none of it had ever happened and when Mum got home Tone-Deaf became a whole other person all over again – hero husband who got his wife a surprise new shower while she was out at work. I sat at the table prodding my sausages with my fork, not saying a word. And when Michaela asked, 'But Daddy, what about the poisonous spider?' he just looked at Angelica and winked. Hero husband with a great sense of humour.

I'd better get back now, I said I'd only be gone an hour. Not that they'll notice, they're so busy looking at the lovely new shower. At least the water's back on again, so I'll be able to wash my yucky hair. Sorry my email's been so gloomy today. Hope you've had another nice day and really sorry to hear about Dylan's accident. Is he OK now? I can't believe he's been electrocuted in real life after what they did to him in Jessop Close!

Love, your e-mate,
Georgie xxx

....

From: nancyblue#@aol.com
To: georgie*harris@hotmail.com
Date: Thur, 3 August 08:08
Subject: Re: Disaster!!!

Dear Georgie,

Are you OK? Has your stepfather ever got violent like that before? Please tell me if it is none of my business, darling, but I'm terribly concerned. I can't bear to think of you being afraid in your own home. And I am cursing the day I ever recommended the wretched oil treatment. What are the odds of the water being switched off the day you decide to do it? I don't know what to say.

It is 8 o'clock in the morning and I am sat up in Bruce's office looking out over the sea. And I am thinking that there is a vastness to both the ocean and sky that has the power to open up and swallow us whole. And although that power can be terrifying at times, at others it can be quite awe-inspiring. The sea is calm this morning – a still, dark sheet spread out before me, reflecting the broken sunshine above. And as I stare out into the deep, shimmering water I wish I could harness its power and send it to you, as one of those email attachment thingies or something, so that you could open it and use it whenever you like. I hope today is better for you, Georgie. I hope that when you wake up you feel sunny and strong again. Please let me know how you are . . .

Lots of love,
Nan xx

Part Three

The Boy with the Sorrowful Smile

From: georgie*harris@hotmail.com
To: nancyblue#@aol.com
Date: Thur, 3 August 19:30
Subject: Weirdness!

Dear Nan,

It's 7 p.m. and guess what? I'm not in the library!!! I decided to go to the internet café on the high street instead. I've had to pay a pound for an hour on a computer but it is so worth it. It's so much more sophisticated than the library. All the staff are dead young and wear tight black jeans and t-shirts. They also have music playing in the background which makes it much more relaxed. I hate the way they're obsessed with silence in the library, it makes me want to jump on a table and sing at the top of my voice, just because I know I'm not supposed to. But in here I can hum along to the music and cough whenever I want. And breathe in the smell of freshly baked cookies to my heart's content. That's another frost-free fact about this place – you are allowed to eat and drink here too, because it's a café as well as an internet place. That's why it's called the internet café!

Anyway, you will be glad to hear that things have been much better today. It was as if that dreaded vegetable oil put a curse on me or something. It's not your fault at all. How were you supposed to know that the council would turn off the water? And please don't be worried about me. I've never seen Tone-Deaf get like that before – well, only the time he broke my Dylan DVD. And there was one time when he couldn't get the top off the ketchup so he smashed the whole bottle in the sink, but I guess that's what you get when you have 'unresolved anger issues', isn't it? He's never ever hurt any of us. He wouldn't dare because like I told you before, he's a typical bully and a big fat coward at heart. And anyway, there's no way Mum would stay with him if he ever hurt me or Michaela. She'd take us somewhere else to live – I know she would.

But I don't want to waste my time talking about Tone-Deaf when I could be telling you about the weird things that happened today. It's quite spooky actually, because although I hadn't read your email until I came here tonight it was as if your thoughts managed to get through to me somehow anyway. Like on some kind of psychic wireless connection. Do you think it's possible that if you think certain thoughts about someone hard enough they will somehow pick up on them? Not read your mind or anything spooky like that, but somehow sense that someone out there wants them to be happy or strong or whatever? I certainly feel a lot stronger today, that's for sure. As soon as my alarm clock went off this morning I sat bolt upright in bed and thought to myself, I am NOT going to have another day like yesterday, whatever happens. So I got up and had a shower – what a luxury, eh! And I have to say that my hair did feel softer than ever before. Mind you I had just given it the world's longest oil treatment lol! (And I AM laughing out loud – because you can laugh as loud as you like in an internet café and no one sssssshhhhs at you!) Anyway, after Angelica had gone to work, and before Tone-Deaf got back, I went into her bedroom and put on some of her lash-volumising mascara and 'frosty pink' lipgloss. Angelica doesn't let me wear make-up unless it's a really special occasion, but after my humiliation yesterday I was determined to look as good as possible today. I decided I was going to 'Dream It, Live It, Be It'; that I was a glamorous actress – just like you ;)

After I'd dried my hair I tried putting it up in a high ponytail but Michaela laughed and said I looked like a pineapple, so I took it down again and just pulled it back loosely, leaving a few strands free at the front. In last month's Mizz magazine they said this was known as the 'Parisian Just-Got-Out-of-Bed look.' It's funny, isn't it, how much work has to go into looking like you've just got out of bed? You have to get up an hour earlier to do it!! Anyway, it turned out really well in the end. Michaela even said I looked 'quite like a princess'.

My plan was to get out of the house before Tone-Deaf got home, but he came back extra early and Michaela was still eating her Coco Pops. He looked at me kind of weird as he walked into the kitchen and said, 'Aye, aye, what's all this then?' I didn't know what he was talking about so I just ignored it and said (all casual), 'I was thinking of taking Michaela to the lido today, as it's so sunny.' (The lido is like this beach that isn't really a beach, near where we live. It has sand and water and stuff, but it isn't the real sea, it's man-made. And Tim Clark from my class went for a swim in it one day and he nearly swallowed a turd, so I don't even put a toe in the water!)

As usual it seemed to take Tone-Deaf ages to reply. And the longer I waited, the more my cheeks burnt, so I pretended to hunt around the cupboard for something so he couldn't see. Then the worst possible thing happened! Michaela started banging her spoon on the table and shouting, 'Liar, liar, pants on fire!' I thought I was going to be puke up my toast and Marmite, I was so scared. 'Who's a liar, Princess?' Tone-Deaf asked. One. Two. Three. Four. I counted the seconds of silence. If it had been a film there would have been one of those big old grandfather clocks ticking away in the corner, its heavy pendulum swinging towards my moment of doom. But Michaela didn't say any more, she just started laughing like Tigger over and over again, 'Hee, hee, hee, hee!'

'OK then,' Tone-Deaf said, and at first I didn't realise he was talking to me, I was so sure I was going to be found out. 'But I want you back by four because you're staying at your nan's tonight.'

What?!!!! 'But how long will we be staying there?' I said, trying really hard not to scream. 'Till tomorrow teatime,' he replied. Then he picked up his newspaper and walked out of the room muttering, 'I'm off to bed.'

Bed? How could he go to bed when my whole life was crashing down around me?!! We wouldn't be coming back till tomorrow teatime! Tone-Deaf's mum lives in East London, at the very opposite end of the Underground. It might as well be the other side of the world. There was no way I'd be able to get to rehearsals tomorrow. And, after I'd messed up my read-through yesterday, Debbie was sure to give my part to someone else.

All the way to the community centre I felt a horrible sliding feeling. Despite my new 'Parisian Just-Got-Out-of-Bed' hair and my volumised eyelashes and glossy lips, inside I felt myself shrinking back to that Carebear-capped disaster of yesterday. What was I going to do? How was I going to break the news to Debbie? I decided to tell her as soon as I got there to get it over with. But before I had the chance to speak to her she gave us all a talk about how hard we were going to have to work to get the show ready in less than three weeks. So I just couldn't do it, she looked too stressed. After that I was so busy I didn't have time to think about tomorrow. Debbie let Michaela play dress-up in the costume cupboard, then she split us into groups to rehearse our different scenes together – which meant I was in a group with Jamie and poor old Jessica was stuck with the dreadful Dred. You should have seen what he was wearing today, his trousers were so low you could see his entire butt sticking out over the top of his waistband. And he had this stupid cap on his head (back to front of course) with 'No. 1 Gangsta' written on it in little shiny studs. 'No. 1 Skanksta' it should have said.

Anyway, the group I was in had to rehearse up on the stage as we were doing the very first scene. We were allowed to read from our scripts (Debbie wants us to have learnt our lines by Monday – gulp!) but we had to start actually acting it out as well this time. Jamie and I were standing offstage while Debbie got the Hoods to do their splurge attack on this boy called Peter who is playing Roxy Robinson. Why couldn't she have given that part to Dred? Then he'd be killed off in the first two minutes! While we were standing in the darkness at the side of the stage Jamie turned to me suddenly and whispered, 'I like your hair.' I was so shocked I didn't know what to say. By the time I managed to say, 'What?' Jamie was reading his first offstage line. But he must have heard me because as soon as he'd said it he turned to me again and said, 'Your hair. I like it like that.' For once it didn't matter that my cheeks went bright red because it was too dark for him to see. No wonder Paris is the city of romance, if this is the reaction they get when they first get out of bed!! Not that I mean Jamie was being romantic or anything, because he wasn't. He was just being nice. Then, just before he walked on stage he looked at me through his long fringe and he gave me another one of his lovely half smiles. I don't know what it is about his smiles but they always give me this really weird feeling inside, like a million little butterflies are having a party in my tummy. I think it's because his smiles look kind of sad, if that makes sense. Anyway, after that I felt so much better and when I came on stage I not only said 'zip the lip' the right way round but I really said it with feeling. I did what you said and have started making notes on my script about how Blousey would really be feeling by each line. I guessed that at the start she would be nervous and tense because she's on her way to an audition. I didn't have too much trouble acting that at all!!

After we'd done our first couple of scenes, Debbie got Jessica's group up on the stage and told me and Jamie to go and practise our scenes together outside. I don't know why, but just her saying that got the butterflies flapping again! Michaela wanted to watch Jessica sing her song so she stayed in the hall with Debbie and I followed Jamie out to the duck pond. Neither of us said a word until he sat down on the grassy bank under the willow tree – although the grass had gone more like straw in all the sunshine. Then he looked up at me and said, 'So?' Like a question. And all I could think to reply was, 'So, what?' Which made me sound like a total idiot, but I didn't know what else to say.

I sat down and pretended to watch the line of ducks slowly gliding across the pond so I could turn my face away from him because, you've guessed it, my cheeks were going bright red again. This wasn't helped by the tropical midday sun. 'So,' he repeated, 'you glad you got Blousey?' Not trusting myself to speak this time I just nodded. 'Me too,' he said. I couldn't help turning to look at him. What did he mean? He was glad I got Blousey or he was glad he got the part he was given? I didn't know what to do, so I just looked back at the pond and the ducks and then, before I could stop myself, I said, 'Makes you think, doesn't it?' I don't know why I said it, because I wasn't really thinking anything, apart from, 'God, why won't my cheeks cool down!'

I heard Jamie shifting around next to me and prayed he would just say yes, like I'd done when he'd said the same thing about the cloud. But no. 'Makes you think what?' he asked. 'The ducks,' I said, unable to think of anything else to say. 'What about them?' he replied. Oh God, it felt as if I'd fallen into the pond and was being dragged down deeper and deeper by a jungle of reeds. 'Well, they make you think, don't they? The ducks,' I said, trying to buy more time. But straight away he replied, 'What do they make you think?' 'About life,' I said, desperate. 'Oh yeah?' he asked. 'Yeah.' I shut my eyes and bit down hard on my lip. Couldn't we just get on with rehearsing? 'So, what do they make you think about life?' Again, I heard Jamie shift around beside me and I turned to see that he had lain down on his side, shading his eyes with his hand as he gazed over to the pond.

I sighed. What did the ducks make me think about life? I desperately wracked my brains and looked back at them. At first they made me think, I wish I had a gun so I could shoot the lot of them for causing so much trouble! But then a memory came flickering back into my head like an old movie. It was of me and my parents and it's one of the few clear memories I have left of dad. We had gone for a picnic in our local park and we were feeding the crusts from our sandwiches to a family of ducks: a mum and a dad and about six little ducklings. I remember my dad giving them all names and talking in their voices as I fed them. He made them say dead silly things like, 'Not for me thanks, I'm on a diet.' Or, 'How dare you throw your stinky old bread at me.' And then my mum joined in, doing the voice of the mother duck and pretending that she was really grand and bossy and wanted all of the bread for herself. Which was even funnier because that's exactly what the mother duck started to do, pushing the dad out of the way so she could get to the bread first.

I took a deep breath and closed my eyes. 'They make me think that no matter how rubbish life can be you've always got your happy memories like a box of precious jewels to keep you smiling,' I said. Then I held my breath and waited for Jamie to laugh or make fun of me. But he didn't do anything and when I plucked up the courage to glance down at him he was still staring at the ducks and he was nodding slowly. As if he really got what I was saying.

After that we went through our lines together, right up until the scene where Bugsy and Blousey have gone on a date. When we got to the line where I have to 'embrace' him I just ignored the stage directions, but then a couple of lines later, when Bugsy kisses his finger and touches Blousey's nose, Jamie actually did it and looked at me really strange, like he was trying to tell me something with his big brown eyes. But right at that moment all of the others came streaming out for lunch so I had to go back in to look after Michaela. I felt really weird. Like something had happened but no one apart from me and Jamie knew it. A bit like when you write a message in invisible ink and only you and the person with the ink highlighter know there's something there. To everyone else it's just a blank piece of paper.

I tried again to tell Debbie that I wouldn't be able to come tomorrow, but she was rushing off to the high street to get some water pistols for the show so I didn't get a chance. And then Jessica and Kate One came in to see me, which I was a little bit surprised about because they normally like to sunbathe and smoke at lunchtime. The first thing Jessica said to me was, 'What have you done to your hair?' And not in a good way. I started to explain about the magazine article but she just smiled and shook her head. 'Never mind,' she said and then she and Kate started talking about who they fancied most at the workshop. It's funny, because before when Jessica talked about Jamie Phelps I always saw him through her eyes, but after today down by the pond he seems like a different person. I suppose we all give other people our own personal definitions, don't we? To Jessica, Jamie is 'like, a total hunk', while I see him as the boy with the sorrowful smile. I didn't tell her that though, I just forced myself to smile and nod as she went on and on about how she wanted to 'snog the face off him'.

It was weird because normally I'm really supportive of Jessica and her diets and her beauty regime and her love life, but today I just wanted to yell at her to shut up, especially because she's still talking in her stupid American accent! Do you think it's possible to outgrow your friends like you outgrow your clothes? Today when I looked at Jessica sitting on the edge of the stage droning on about Jamie she reminded me of this red velvet party dress I had when I was a little girl. It had these great big plastic jewels sewn on to the hem and when I first saw it I thought it was so lovely and grown up but now it just seems silly and over the top.

After lunch, Debbie wanted to work on the song and dance routines, so it was mega busy and the afternoon flew by. I got to sing Ordinary Fool right at the end, but this time I didn't feel nearly as nervous. I just looked over at Jamie before I started because I knew he was going to give me another one of his smiles. And again I felt as if I'd been given a secret sign that only I could read and it made me feel so strong. Didn't you love singing that song when you played Blousey? It is so full of meaning, isn't it? All I had to do was think of my sad life and all of the dreams I've had that have fallen through and I nearly made myself cry when I sang it. When I finished Debbie gave me a hug and said well done so I figured that was as good a time as any to tell her I wouldn't be able to come tomorrow. Plus it was 3.55 so it was then or never! When I first told her, everyone went silent – waiting for her to go nuts probably – but she wasn't cross at all. And she didn't give my part to anyone else. She did ask if there was any way I could meet up with Jamie over the weekend to practise our scenes though!! I didn't know what to say and I didn't look anywhere near Jessica that's for sure. But then I heard Jamie say, 'Yeah, no problem,' so I just nodded. And then Debbie said, 'That's it for today,' so we all got up to go.

Jessica and the two Kates came straight over the minute we finished and Jessica was smiling this really weird smile, as if someone was forcing the corners of her mouth up with a crowbar. 'Why can't you come tomorrow, George?' she said, and her words sounded as forced as her smile. 'I have to go to my stepdad's mum's house,' I replied, collecting up Michaela's toys. 'Can't you tell him it's important?' Jessica hissed back at me. 'Can't you tell him that you need to rehearse?' I shook my head. And then I had a genius idea. I'd tell her the truth and then she'd feel sorry for me and realise I had no choice. And she wouldn't be mad at me for having to have a private rehearsal with Jamie. 'My parents don't even know I'm coming here,' I whispered. There, I thought, that ought to do it. Normally Jessica is the one lying to her parents; surely she would be impressed to hear that I was being dishonest for once? But instead of throwing her head back and laughing or putting her arm round me and giving me a hug (as I had kind of hoped she would) she just stared at me. Then she looked at the two Kates. Her pretend smile had totally disappeared.

'Are you serious?' she finally said, looking back at me and shaking her head. There was something about the way she was looking at me that reminded me of Tone-Deaf and I felt my cheeks go red and my eyes start to burn and for a split second I thought I was going to cry. I am so sick of being spoken to as if I am a complete idiot who can't get anything right. But then I felt someone touch me on the shoulder and I turned round and saw Jamie and he was holding out a scrap of paper. 'Here's my number,' he said in his gruff voice. 'Give us a ring Saturday morning and we'll meet up.' But before I could reply he'd gone. I looked at the piece of paper and then I looked at Jessica and all of a sudden I wanted to laugh not cry. Because somehow, on this weirdest of weird days, I had managed to get the phone number of the boy she has loved for two whole years! And I know I haven't got his number because he likes me or because we're going on a date or anything like that, but it was so nice to have got something that Jessica wants for once. I don't think Jessica could believe what had happened either. The way her eyes kept flitting back and forth it was as if she didn't know whether to go after Jamie or stay with me – and the precious phone number. I picked up Michaela's bag and took her by the hand. 'Come on, Michaela, we have to go,' I said, and we walked right out of there, leaving Jessica and the two Kates standing like a bowl of goldfishes gulping in shock.

So there you have it – my weird day. Thank you so much for your email and all those lovely things you said about the sea and sending its power to me. It is so nice to think that there's someone out there – who I've never even met – who really cares about what happens to me.

At school they're always going on about stranger danger and chatting to people you don't know online. And I understand why they do it. I know there are bad people out there. And I know I don't really know you and I've never even met, or spoken, to you. And I know my teachers would probably say I shouldn't be emailing you because you're still a stranger. But I am 14 years old. I'm not a little kid. I can be trusted to make my own choices. And I'm so glad I chose to become e-mates with you.

I won't be able to email you tomorrow as I'll be at Tone-Deaf's mum's. It's funny because before I would have been so depressed at missing rehearsals to go there but now, with Jamie's number in my pocket, I feel as if I've been given a magic crystal with super powers! All I need to do is touch it or look at it and I feel amazing.

Lots of love,
Georgie xxx

....

From: nancyblue#@aol.com
To: georgie*harris@hotmail.com
Date: Fri, 4 August 10:03
Subject: Re: Weirdness

Dear Georgie,

Well, thank goodness for that. I am so pleased things are looking up again. And I am so glad you liked my last email.

I have to admit it has crossed my mind that our email friendship might be considered a little 'out of the ordinary'. One hears such horrible stories of unsavoury characters using the internet to trick young people. And for the most terrible reasons. I know that when we first communicated I was pretending to be Dylan. But you know why that was and you know who I am now. And, as a supposedly responsible adult (laugh out VERY loud!), I have attached a recent photo of myself and Dylan, taken in the garden here in Hove. Just so that you can rest assured you are emailing a little old lady and not some kind of hideous bogeyman. I also thought you might like a private picture of Dylan for your collection ;)

Well, what a day you have had indeed! Your new hairstyle sounds delightful and yes, I guess it must be the most moisturised hair in Britain right now! Can I say something darling, and please ignore me if it's none of my business, but do you think Jessica could be jealous of you? I only ask because it very much seems that way to an outsider reading between the lines. So don't let her upset you. Better to be envied than pitied I always say, and believe me, I've encountered more than my fair share of sniping, petty females. The acting world is full of them, my dear, so you'd better get used to it!!

Moving on to more pleasant matters, I must say that Jamie Phelps sounds quite intriguing. The boy with the sorrowful smile. Hmm, what could lie behind that, I wonder. As an actor you do tend to become fascinated by people and what makes them tick – it's all that 'getting into character' and working out their motivations. You must know what I'm talking about now you are working on Blousey. What makes the mysterious Jamie tick, I wonder? Oh well, no doubt you'll get to the bottom of it this weekend. Cannot wait to hear your next update and hope your visit to Tone-Deaf's mother's isn't too gruelling. Isn't she the one who chews with her mouth open and says 'stone the crows' all the time?

I'm off to a poetry class now – all part of my 'show must go on' effort. Can't write for love nor money but what the hell, I'll give it a go.

Lots of love,
Nan xx

PS: There was a young girl from Ruislip
    Who . . .

Damn it, I can't even write a limerick for you. What the hell rhymes with Ruislip? Why couldn't you have lived in Wales or Kent?

From: georgie*harris@hotmail.com
To: nancyblue#@aol.com
Date: Sat, 5 August 09:22
Subject: Stone Me!

There was an old lady from Mile End
Whose step-granddaughter she sent round the bend
All she said was 'stone me'
As she chewed on toffee
And read the tea leaves for her friend.

Hi Nan,

THANK YOU SO MUCH FOR THE PHOTO!!! You
didn't have to send it – I do trust you, you know – but I'm
so glad you did. You both look really lovely.

I have just popped into the library on my way to meet Jamie
for our rehearsal. OMG I am so nervous. I know this isn't a
date or anything but it is probably the closest I'll get to one
in my sad lifetime. My 'Parisian Just-Got-Out-of-Bed' hair
is a disaster, more like 'Just-Got-Dragged-Through-a-
Bush', and I wasn't able to put on any make-up because
Angelica is at home, and being all lovey-dovey with Tone-
Deaf since their day alone without us kids, which is making
me want to PUKE!! Oh well, at least for once I haven't got

143

Michaela with me. Am meeting Jamie at the bus station in 5 mins so better go. Hope your poetry class went well. The limerick above is about Tone-Deaf's mum, in case you didn't guess. It's very considerate of her to live somewhere that rhymes with 'round the bend', don't you think?

Georgie xxxx

....

From: nancyblue#@aol.com
To: georgie*harris@hotmail.com
Date: Sat, 5 August 13:47
Subject: Re: Stone Me

Oooh, darling, I can't wait to hear how you get on. I know it isn't a date but it certainly sounds as if there's a spark between you and Jamie. I loved the way you put it – a message in invisible ink that only you two can see. Oh, I wish I could write like that! The poetry class was a disaster – and, quite frankly, full of freaks! Does one have to be insane to be a poet? Or anaemic? Or think that beads, wellington boots and a bra worn over the top of one's tie-dye t-shirt is a good look? I thought *actors* were supposed to be eccentric! The whole point of me joining classes and getting back into the swing of things was to cheer myself up. Two hours spent in a drafty (even in this heatwave) basement room in a library, listening to Brighton's living dead read dirge after dirge about depression and solitude, and even on one occasion the cold-blooded murder of a baby, really did not do it for me, I can tell you. I may as well have spent a couple of hours at the local mortuary watching all the corpses being wheeled in.

But enough of this misery. I hope you are having a lovely day, darling, and I cannot wait to hear how your rehearsal goes.

Lots of love,
Nan xx

PS: There was a YOUNG woman from Hove
    Who lived in a pebbly cove.
    She tried being a poet
    But wouldn't you know it
    To suicide, her, it drove.

That last line isn't grammatically correct, is it? See, I told you, I don't have a poetic bone in my body.

From: georgie*harris@hotmail.com
To: nancyblue#@aol.com
Date: Sat, 5 August 19:14
Subject: OH MY GODDDDDDDDDDDDDD!!!

Oh Nan. Oh my God! I am back in the internet café, it's 7.10 at night and I can't stop laughing. Good job I'm not in the library, eh? You will not believe what has happened.

OK, take a deep breath Georgie, and calm down! I don't know where to begin and I know you hate the way I always take so long to get to that denouement thing so I'll begin with the end – I think I've got a date!! And, no I don't mean one of those horrible shrivelled-up dried fruits. I think I've got a DATE, date. With Jamie. Well, I suppose it depends on how you define date really. But I have spent most of the day with him and now I'm on my way to meet him again. Because he's asked me to come out with him tonight – and that's normally a date, isn't it? When a boy asks you to go out with him and it isn't to rehearse your lines or study or something sad like that. The thing is, it isn't quite like the dates you read about in books or see on the telly. We're not going to the cinema or for a pizza or anything. And there are going to be other people there as well, so it won't just be us two. Hmm, I think I need to list it. That's what Angelica tells me to do whenever I'm in a dilemma about

146

something – make a list of all the reasons for and against. So here goes:

PROOF TONIGHT IS A DATE:
Jamie asked me if I'd like to go out with him tonight – in those exact words.
He was giving me one of his lovely sorrowful smiles when he did it – and he stroked the side of my face with his thumb. Actually that's another point in it's own right – he stroked my face with his thumb and it felt really romantic.

PROOF TONIGHT IS NOT A DATE AND I AM JUST A SAD DESPERADO:
We are going to Mad Bess Woods – not the cinema or Pizza Hut or any other typical date venue.
Other people are going to be there – Jamie's band-mates and friends.
We are going for a 'jamming session' around the fire. Is that really a date activity?

OK, so maybe it's not a date after all, but I am going out with Jamie and I have just had THE most amazing day of my life. I'm meeting him at 8 o'clock down by the war memorial but first I have got to let you know what happened today. So here's the beginning of my story.

When I met him at the bus station earlier I felt well embarrassed. It's weird isn't it, when you see someone in a different place or situation to what you're used to. One time, when I was about Michaela's age, I saw my teacher Miss Baldwin when I was out ice-skating with my mum and dad. She was with a man with a big brown beard and she was wearing loads of make-up and gold jewellery and I remember I saw them kissing by the side of the rink and I was so shocked to see her doing something like that I wanted to cry. Up until that point I don't think I realised teachers had a life outside of school. I suppose I must have thought they tucked themselves away in a cupboard with the paints and the books after we had all gone home. But anyway, I remember feeling really embarrassed when I saw her and that's exactly how I felt today, seeing Jamie standing there at the bus station in his jeans and hooded sweatshirt. He looked older, outside of school and the drama workshop, and for a split second I thought about jumping on the bus that was waiting there and leaving without him seeing me. But I didn't get the chance because before I could do anything I heard him shout out, 'Hey, Blousey, what's happening?' And then I couldn't help smiling even though, surprise, surprise, my cheeks had begun to burn.

I read in a magazine once that to avoid your cheeks going red you have to imagine really hard that you are freezing cold. Well, today as I walked towards Jamie I was imagining I was a naked Eskimo, trapped under an avalanche, eating an ice-pop, but it still didn't make any difference. My cheeks still flushed as if I was wearing a fur hat and coat and eating a curry in the Sahara desert! It turned out that the bus waiting at the stop was the one we needed to get to Jamie's house. I couldn't believe he wanted us to go to his house! I thought we'd just go to the park or something. Jamie lives in a place called Ickenham, which is like this small village-type place just outside of Ruislip. (It isn't really a village as it's still in London and has a tube station and a busy main road but it does have a little green by the shops and a really old pub called the Coach and Horses that still has a railing outside to tie your horses to!) Jamie's house is on a road just behind the pub and it's amazing. Not because it's a big posh mansion or anything – in fact it's a council house, or was, I think his parents own it now. From the outside it looks pretty normal, semi-detached with a little front garden that's paved over and full of motorbikes. His dad is a motorbike mechanic. Normally it makes me sad when I see a bike because it reminds me of my dad and how he died, but not today. Today it felt kind of homely seeing the bikes and the engine parts and the oil. It made me think of our old flat in Kilburn and the yard around the back where my dad kept his bike.

But it's the inside of Jamie's house that's the best. Oh Nan, I wish I had some photos I could send you, you'd love it. As soon as you walk in it's like going back to the olden days, you know, when they had flower power and all that hippy stuff. Everywhere is painted in really bright colours – the hall is turquoise with big blue swirly patterns. I know that probably sounds gross but it looks great, trust me. The kitchen and living room open on to each other, so the downstairs looks really big. The kitchen walls are covered in tiny multicoloured tiles so it's like standing inside a gigantic mosaic and there's this rack full of millions of different herbs and spices that smells just like the health-food shop. The living room is painted dark green and there are loads of these really frost-free pictures hanging on the walls. They're the kind of pictures where at first when you look at them all you see are patterns but the longer you look the more they come to life. A bit like those tests they do on crazy people where they give them pictures and ask them what they see and if they say a vase of flowers they are sane but if they say a severed head they are a psycho. I wonder what Tone-Deaf would see – ha, ha!!

There was one picture I really loved. It was the size of a really large flat-screen telly and it reminded me of the ocean – all green and blue and covered with little metallic dashes that looked just like fishes darting in and out of waves. I asked Jamie what it was supposed to be and when he didn't reply I turned round and saw he was looking at the floor, his long fringe completely covering his face. 'The picture,' I said, thinking he maybe didn't understand what I meant. Then he looked up and guess what? His cheeks were bright red! 'What do you think it is?' he muttered, looking away from me, towards the window. I turned back to the picture. 'I think it's the ocean,' I replied. And then I thought of your email about the sea. 'And I think it's about the power and mystery of the sea and how we think we understand it, but really we don't have a clue about the creatures that live down there or what it is really capable of.' I had to stay looking at the picture then because my own cheeks were blushing. Why can't I ever give a straight forward answer to his questions? Why do I always have to drone on like an idiot? At least I didn't say I thought it was a severed head though lol!! But it was fine because then he came over to where I was standing and he told me that his mum had painted it and that it was the sea and that she would be really pleased I had got it.

We spent about an hour working on Bugsy Malone and then Jamie's mum got home from work. She works in a tattoo parlour in Ruislip Manor, designing tattoos! And she is REALLY nice. Jamie told her I liked her picture and she gave me a massive hug and called me 'honey'. It was all so different to what I was expecting. For a start, I was not expecting to go round to his house. And secondly, I had expected him to have a horrible family. I don't know why – his sorrowful smile perhaps?! But his mum is lovely and although I didn't meet his dad he sounds really nice too. The way his mum talks about him, calling him her grease monkey, you can tell she really loves him. Jamie has two older brothers, but neither of them lives at home anymore. One is married with two kids around Michaela's age and lives up in Stevenage and the other one is off backpacking around Asia.

So anyway, after we did some rehearsing – oh Nan, this time when he kissed his finger and touched my nose it was like he'd pressed the control switch for the butterflies in my tummy and set them on to fast forward! Anyway after that we had some lunch. Donna, Jamie's mum, made us bacon and sausage sandwiches on this really delicious fluffy white bread. And then Jamie asked if I'd like to see his room. At that point I have to admit that I felt a little sick. I've never been in a boy's room before – well, not an older boy who has such an effect on my cheeks and stomach anyway. I didn't know what to say so I just followed him upstairs, my heart and the butterflies fluttering away like mad, but it was fine. When we got up there he showed me his guitars. He has two – a blue acoustic and a white electric

– and he played me a couple of songs. And then we watched the DVD of – oh, I can't remember the title – all I know is it was about a gang of idiot bank robbers who keep messing everything up but somehow manage to come out all right in the end. Watching that movie was a bit like trying to read a book when you've just been told the most amazing piece of news ever. You try and focus on the characters and the plot but all the time they're being drowned out by a voice in your head shouting about other stuff. In this case the voice kept saying, 'OH MY GOD. YOU ARE SITTING ON A BED WITH JAMIE PHELPS. YOU ARE SITTING ON JAMIE PHELPS' BED.' And then, 'OH GOD, WE'RE SO CLOSE WE'RE ALMOST TOUCHING.' And then, 'WE ARE TOUCHING!'

It was only our arms brushing against each other but I thought I was going to die. Now I know what they mean in Tone-Deaf's mum's romance books when they talk about 'little pulses of electricity charging straight to Violet's (or whatever the sappy heroine is called) most intimate places!' Thankfully I didn't die though. Not even when I said I ought to be going and he looked at me with those big brown eyes and smiled that smile and said, 'Would you like to come out with me tonight?' Or when he brought his thumb up to the side of my face and traced it as gently as a breeze down my cheek.

And so here I am – 10 minutes before I have to meet him again. I told my mum I was going out with Jessica. It worked out brilliantly because apparently Jessica had been phoning for me all afternoon. Hmm, I wonder why?!! And my mum was in one of her mega-happy moods so she was totally cool about me coming out. She even said I could stay out till 11 when I told her we were going to the cinema. When I rang Jessica back I said I couldn't speak because I was going straight out to a family meal. She wasn't happy, but at least it will stop her ringing tonight and giving the game away. So I'm off now. Wish me luck!

Lots of love,
Georgie xxx

....

From: nancyblue#@aol.com
To: georgie*harris@hotmail.com
Date: Sat, 5 August 23:57
Subject: Re: OH MY GODDDDDDDDDDDDDDD!!!

Well, well, well – a date, eh? I just knew something was going to happen. I said to Woodstock, when it finally got cool enough to walk him this evening, 'Love is in the air'

– in Ruislip at least. Oh, darling, this is so exciting. As for is it a date or isn't it? To me it sounds very much as if he likes you – why else would he ask you to come to his house? Or ask you to come out with him and his friends tonight? Or stroke your face with his thumb? Date or not, it's all terribly thrilling.

It's 5-to-midnight now so I guess you must be back at home, tucked up in bed and reliving every moment of today over and over in your head. At least if you are anything like I used to be. First dates are so exciting – a cocktail of fear and joy with a shot of attraction and a sprinkling of anticipation all thrown in. And they either leave you drunk on love or hungover with disappointment. Hopefully yours will be the former, obviously! How was that for a metaphor? I'm thinking of resurrecting my epic writing career from the ashes of the poetry wake and enrolling on a scriptwriting course at the local night school. I also have to say, please, please, please, Georgie darling, can you refrain from referring to the 60s as 'the olden days'! You make me feel like a dinosaur!

Do let me know how you got on, sweetie, as soon as possible! Am going to attempt to get some sleep now. Have taken to sleeping on the sofa in Bruce's study the past couple of nights – the sound of the waves are as soothing as a lullaby and sometimes, if I listen hard enough, I can hear Bruce whispering to me on the breeze.

Goodnight and God bless,
Nan xx

....

From: georgie*harris@hotmail.com
To: nancyblue#@aol.com
Date: Sun, 6 August 15:13
Subject: The best of times and worst of times

Oh Nan, Charles Dickens could have been writing about me when he said, 'it was the best of times, it was the worst of times'. Why can't life ever just be somewhere in the middle: not too good, not too crap? And stay that way. When I was little it wasn't like this. At least I don't think it was. The trouble is my memories of back then seem to be getting more and more unclear, like photos fading in the sun. And I hate that because it's like I'm losing what little I have left of my dad a bit more every day. Sorry, I'm trying really hard not to cry but my eyes feel as if they're full to the brim with tears and at any moment there's going to be a mini tsunami all down my face. I liked your first-date cocktail metaphor by the way. It was really true. Only in my case last night you would have had to add an extra big shot of humiliation as well, if it had been a date, which it so clearly wasn't, as it turned out. I haven't got long because guess what? I'm at the stupid library and it's only open until 4 on a Sunday and it's just gone 3 already. To be honest, I nearly didn't come at all. I had a feeling you'd want to know all about my so-called date and I really didn't want to have to tell you the awful truth. But here goes . . .

When I got to the war memorial Jamie was sitting on the bottom step, his guitar case propped next to him, looking up at the names of all the dead soldiers. 'Some of these were only a year older than me,' he said, as I walked over. I felt a little pang of sorrow as I looked up at the lists of names engraved into the grey stone. It felt weird imagining boys like Jamie going off to fight and die in a war. It made me shiver. As if he could read my mind, Jamie stood up and gave me a hug. It only lasted a second and now I know what was going to happen later it makes me squirm, but at the time it felt so nice. He felt so strong and his aftershave smelt delicious, like a forest after it's been raining. 'You all right, Blousey?' he said, reaching to stroke my face like he'd done in his bedroom. I didn't trust myself to speak, I felt so sure my voice would come out in a high-pitched squeak, so I just nodded. But it was great because right away we were back where we had left off and there was no awkwardness at all. On the way to the woods, Jamie told me all about his band and how the other members were all older and had left school and that he couldn't wait to leave next September either – he hates being told what to do and where to be. Oh, it's so hard to write about all the nice stuff now, knowing what was going on behind the scenes.

Anyway, Jamie asked all about what I wanted to do when I left school, or 'escaped' as he put it. And it was so nice to be with someone who actually seemed interested in me. And he was really interested when I told him my dad used to be a roadie. He said he thought I was a really cool singer and that was why he had invited me out with him because he wanted his band-mates to hear my voice. So you see, it wasn't a date – it never had been. I really don't know why I thought it could have been. But anyway, at that point I wasn't too disappointed, because at that point I didn't know I was walking towards the worst night of my life.

When we got to the woods Jamie led me to this really cool part I'd never been to before. You have to go scrambling through some bushes for about 5 minutes and then you come to this clearing. Apparently in the Second World War the government built a secret underground bomb shelter there, but now it's just a perfect circle of mossy earth, walled by trees. Jamie's mates were already there when we arrived and they were trying to get a fire going. There are four other members of the band – a really thin boy called Karl, who plays the bass, a really big boy called Honey Monster who plays the drums, Tez, who plays keyboards and sax, and Pete, who plays guitar. Jamie also plays guitar and he's their lead singer. Karl and Tez had brought their girlfriends with them so thankfully I wasn't the only girl. But it was really embarrassing at first, having to sit there while Jamie introduced me. 'This is Blousey,' he said, 'the one I've been telling you about.' That was the joy part of my 'first-date cocktail' – when they all turned to smile at me and Honey Monster said, 'Ah yes, the girl with the awesome voice.' (Hmm – and the bright scarlet cheeks of course!) But I was so happy at that moment I didn't care that it hadn't turned out to be a date. Jamie had actually told them about me! And he had obviously said really nice things about my singing!

Once they got the fire going the boys all opened cans of beer and Karl's girlfriend passed me a bottle of wine and a plastic cup. She was tanned and slim and wearing really pretty silvery eyeshadow that glimmered in the firelight. For a split second I thought about taking the wine, just to save the embarrassment, but I couldn't do it. So I shook my head and muttered, 'Sorry, I don't drink.' But instead of laugh at me or look at me like I was some kind of freak, the girl just smiled and Jamie reached inside his bag and handed me a can of Coke. It was so nice to realise that it was OK for me to just be me for once and not have to pretend to be cool or sophisticated or anything else. Then Jamie and Pete started strumming on their guitars and Jamie gave me one of his lovely smiles – which looked even nicer with the shadows from the flames flickering about his face – and he said, 'How about a song, Blousey?' At first I was hoping he meant did I want him to play me a request, but then Honey Monster said, 'Yeah, let's hear this killer voice then.' My heart started to pound, but Jamie started playing a few chords and I recognised them immediately. He was playing the intro to Wonderful Tonight – my dad's song to my mum! So I just stared into the flames until it felt like everything else had melted away into gold and all I could hear was Jamie's guitar. And I realised that it must have been exactly how my dad's guitar sounded all those years ago to my mum. And then I started to sing. Softly at first but then louder and stronger. And it was as if I was in that hotel room in Manchester, watching my mum watching my dad as his fingers gently strummed the strings as he sang those beautiful words to her. A tear spilled over the rim of my eye and trickled down my face. But it felt nice. Like it was washing the pain away or something. When I finished singing I kept staring into the fire. Then Honey Monster let out a whoop and they all started clapping really loudly and Jamie put down his guitar and put his hand over mine. I looked up at him but this time he wasn't smiling, he was just staring at me. And then it happened. The worst night of my life began.

'Hello, George.' We all turned around and there, at the entrance to the clearing, stood Jessica and Kate One and Dred. I didn't know what to be the most shocked at. That Jessica and Kate were there, or that they were with Dred. The first thing I thought was, Jessica never goes down to the woods. She's always said they're full of pervs in dirty raincoats who like to show their you-know-whats to school-girls.

'What are you doing?' Jessica asked, looking straight at me. I felt Jamie's hand slip away from mine, as quickly and smoothly as a silk glove. 'I, er, I'm having a jamming session,' I finally replied. When Jamie had talked about having a jamming session earlier it had sounded cool and grown-up, but when I said it I just sounded like a stupid kid. 'Oh. Right,' Jessica said and then she walked over to me. 'Room for any more,' she said in a sickly sweet voice, looking straight down at Jamie. She was wearing her tightest jeans, with a little strappy top showing off her toned stomach and her long blonde hair shining like a shaft of sunshine on her back. 'Yeah, sure,' Jamie replied gruffly. And the next thing I knew Jessica had plonked herself down right between me and Jamie and then Kate One and Dred came over and asked me to budge up, so that in the end all three of them were sat between us.

'How did you know we were here?' Jamie asked. 'George told me,' Jessica replied. 'What? When?' I said, leaning forward to stare at her. 'On the phone earlier,' Jessica continued in her voice as sickly as candyfloss, 'when you rang to invite us.' I sat there for a moment, motionless. What was she talking about? I hadn't invited her. I'd said that I was going out for a family dinner. It took about a minute for the reality to sink in – they must have followed me. I felt numb with shock. But I knew there was no point in me denying what she'd said. Jessica is such an expert at lying she could have a university degree in it. I've been there when she's been convincing her mum that she's been studying at the library when really she's been snogging a boy behind the toilets in the park or shoplifting make-up from Superdrug. I know how good she is. And in that moment I went from feeling like I was in the perfect place, at the perfect time, with the perfect people, to feeling like I was in the worst place in the world. All I wanted was for the ground to open up and transport me down to that Second World War bomb shelter. Maybe then I'd be able to escape from the embarrassment. But of course it didn't and instead I had to sit there in silence, listening to Jessica shrieking and flirting with Jamie and watching as Kate One and Dred started to snog. And I felt so ashamed. Although they didn't say anything, I could see Jamie's friends shooting glances across the fire at each other, like secret text messages:

WHO THE HELL R THESE PEOPLE?
WHY DID THAT STUPID KID HAVE 2 INVITE THEM?

And I wanted to die because none of it was my fault, but they would never know the truth. Honey Monster was nice though, he called across to me, 'Hey Blousey, you've got one hell of a voice.' But this only made things a million times worse because then Jessica immediately piped up, 'Ooh, I could sing something if you like?' And, before anyone had the chance to reply, she started singing Flying without Wings. But instead of looking cool like she always does at school she looked stupid and childish and all the secret text messages started flying around the fire again:

WHO DOES SHE THINK SHE IS?
THIS ISN'T AN AUDITION FOR X-FACTOR

Tez's girlfriend even started to giggle when Jessica sang a

really high note and kept it going for about an hour. When she finished no one clapped or said anything and the silence was painful. Jessica soon found a way to fill it though. 'So, George, we called round at your house before.' My heart didn't just sink, it plummeted right to the very bottom of the underground shelter. Unfortunately it didn't take the rest of my body with it. 'You went round to my house? What, tonight?' I asked, my voice like a mouse's squeak. Jessica nodded. I saw Jamie lean forward to stare at me. 'Yes,' Jessica continued. 'Your mum was in a right state.' Next to me, Dred let out a snort of laughter.

There's something I have to tell you Nan, before I go on. About my mum. I think I said before, that my mum gets ill sometimes. Well, the thing is I wasn't being strictly truthful with you. She does get ill, but it's because she has this other problem you see – a drink problem. I didn't want to tell you because I haven't told anyone, apart from Jessica, and that was in the strictest confidence because one night I just couldn't take it any more and I had to tell someone. Angelica's not an alcoholic or anything. She doesn't have to have a drink every day, or keep a bottle of vodka in a brown paper bag under her bed or anything like that. But sometimes, when everything gets too much for her, she has to get drunk – really drunk – and I hate it. Because although she sometimes gets funny and giggly and happy, like she used to be when my dad was alive, most times she ends up crying and being sick and I have to clean it all up and look after her. And Tone-Deaf hates it and he shouts at her and calls her names and I can't bear it. A few months ago, when Angelica was really drunk, Jessica rang me and she could tell something was wrong. So I ended up spilling it all out to her, about how Angelica had been sick all over the kitchen floor and I was fed-up of feeling like I was the mum and she was the kid. Jessica was really nice at the time, saying she couldn't believe it and how awful it was and how brave I was for dealing with it.

But she didn't say any of that stuff last night. No, last night, around the fire, in front of Jamie and all his friends and Kate One and the horrible Dred, she talked about how drunk my mum had been when she'd gone round to call for me and how Michaela had been crying. And then she asked me how I could have gone out and left a little four year-old with someone so wrecked and if that had been her she would never have left her brother. Then she said I was lucky no one had ever called the social services and we hadn't been taken into care. It felt as if a million little arrows poisoned with horrible thoughts came flying at me through the trees and stabbing into my brain. Jessica had been to my house. She had seen my mum drunk. She must have told Angelica we weren't going to the cinema. She must have told her I'd lied. And Michaela was crying and I wasn't there to comfort her. Somebody might call social services. Michaela and I could get taken into care.

Somehow I managed to stumble to my feet and mutter something about having to go. Tears were spilling down my face and I couldn't remember where the entrance to the clearing was. 'Sorry,' I kept saying over and over again as I tripped over a guitar and someone's bag. 'Sorry.' And I did feel so sorry – for ever coming out in the first place. For actually daring to think that I could do something really fun and exciting for once. For actually daring to think that I could have been going on a date with Jamie. I didn't look anywhere near his direction as I made my way around the circle and finally found the gap in the trees. I heard him call out 'Wait,' but I just ignored him and scrambled out of there as fast as I could. I think he might have tried coming after me. I heard him calling again and some noise in the bushes behind me, but I kept going and didn't stop until I got back home.

The one good thing about what happened was that I got back nice and early. Tone-Deaf was still at the pub and Angelica had fallen asleep on the sofa. I washed her glass and emptied the ashtray and hid the empty bottle in the outside bin and then I woke her and helped her up to bed.

Luckily she was too out of it to remember that Jessica had been round. When I went into my room Michaela was asleep in my bed, clutching on to my teddy bear, Hendrix. The front of her hair was wet and tangled from where she had been crying.

So now you know the whole sad story. I hope you don't think I'm too horrible. I don't normally leave Michaela with my mum when she's like that but I just wanted to be a normal teenager for once. And do normal teenage stuff. Please don't be mad at me. I don't know what I'd do if I didn't have you to talk to. Well, if I didn't have you to email, but it's like talking, isn't it? I'd hate it if I lost you on top of everything else.

Now I'm crying again. I'd better go. Sorry.

Georgie xx

....

From: georgie*harris@hotmail.com
To: nancyblue#@aol.com
Date: Mon, 7 August 09:01
Subject: Hello

Hi Nan,

I came to the library as soon as it opened this morning because I was hoping you might have sent me a mail last night. But all I had in my inbox was one of those spams telling me a prince in Burkina Faso wants to pay 6 million dollars into my account. Oh, if only! Are you mad at me? Please could you just send me an email and tell me what you're thinking? I couldn't bear it if you didn't email me anymore. Everything's fine at home now. Angelica didn't have a drink at all yesterday and Tone-Deaf was out all day with his mates so it was lovely and quiet. Mum even did a puppet show with Michaela. So you see it really isn't that bad. I'm sorry if you are mad at me and I promise I won't leave Michaela with Angelica when she's you-know-what ever again. Please email me.

Lots of love,
Georgie xx

From: nancyblue#@aol.com
To: georgie*harris@hotmail.com
Date: Mon, 7 August 16:02
Subject: One hundred million apologies!!

Oh Georgie, darling, of course I'm not mad at you! Why on earth would I be and what on earth do you have to apologise for? I'm the one who should be apologising to you for not getting back to you sooner. And I'm so, so sorry. I had a bit of a mini crisis of my own yesterday and I didn't turn my computer on. Didn't even get out of bed. Poor Woodstock had to make do with the back garden for his walks I'm afraid. I wasn't going to do anything today either. Honestly, it was like a thick fog of gloom had rolled in off the sea and set itself down upon me. But strangely enough a little voice in my head kept telling me to have a quick check of my emails. And I am so glad it did. I was really shocked when I read your message because I'd been certain you were going to have a fabulous night. To be honest I wasn't really sure if I'd be getting many more emails from you. Things between you and Jamie seemed to be going so well. And I remember what it's like when you're in the throes of a new romance, you have no time for anything else. Well, I can vaguely remember anyhow!

I'm so sorry you had such a terrible night. This computer is extremely frustrating, there's so much I want to say to you but all I have in front of me are stupid letters on a stupid screen. I'd love to be able to reach through my computer somehow and give you a hug and tell you that everything is going to be OK. I wonder if you're online now. It's just gone 4 o'clock so you might have called into the library on your way home from the drama workshop. I do hope you went today despite what happened at the weekend. It would be an awful thing to let that walking crab stick win. I'm going to send this right now just in case you are online and then maybe we could send emails quickly back and forth, as if we were having a real conversation? I'll keep my computer on for the next half an hour and keep checking.

All my love,
Nan xx

....

From: georgie*harris@hotmail.com
To: nancyblue#@aol.com
Date: Mon, 7 August 16:06
Subject: I'm here!!

Oh my God! I just got your mail! I'm in the library. Will send this message now to let you know, then send a more detailed one.

G xx

....

From: nancyblue#@aol.com
To: georgie*harris@hotmail.com
Date: Mon, 7 August 16:08
Subject: Re: I'm here!!

Hurrah!! We have communication! How are you, darling? Did you go to the workshop today? Please tell me you did?

Nan xx

....

From: georgie*harris@hotmail.com
To: nancyblue#@aol.com
Date: Mon, 7 August 16:11
Subject: Re: I'm here!!

Hi,

Yes, I did. Didn't want to — obviously! But when I told Michaela we wouldn't be going she started to cry and I was so guilty about leaving her on Saturday night I told her OK. Even if it meant enduring the shame of seeing Jessica and Jamie again. It was weird though, because part of me didn't care. It's as if the humiliation of Saturday night has left me numb. My dad had a friend called Roger, another roadie, and when he was a kid he'd had an electric shock and it left him with no feeling in his left arm. When he was drunk he used to put cigarettes out on his skin because he couldn't feel a thing. That's how my heart is now — totally and utterly numb. I don't think anything could ever hurt it again. It all turned out fine at the workshop anyway, because Jessica wasn't even there!

G xx

From: nancyblue#@aol.com
To: georgie*harris@hotmail.com
Date: Mon, 7 August 16:13
Subject: Re: I'm here!!

Oh how wonderful! I'm so pleased you went – and dare I
ask about Jamie? Was he there? How did it go? How are you
feeling now?

Nan xx

....

From: georgie*harris@hotmail.com
To: nancyblue#@aol.com
Date: Mon, 7 August 16:15
Subject: Re: I'm here!!

No, he wasn't. I don't care though. I'd rather not see him
after what happened on Saturday. I guess he and Jessica
must have finally got it together after I left. They were
probably out on a proper date today. She was probably
round at his house having lunch with his mum, eating crab
stick sandwiches. But I'm OK about it, honest. After what
happened on Saturday I've realised that I can't even think

about going out or romance or any of that stuff – not while my mum is the way she is. I have to take care of her and Michaela. That's what my dad would have wanted me to do, and anyway me and boys and romance always seems to end in total shame. I still haven't forgotten about Dylan you know! I have to realise that it just isn't going to happen to me. I'm way too ugly and dull and stupid for any boy to really like me.

Gxx

....

From: nancyblue#@aol.com
To: georgie*harris@hotmail.com
Date: Mon, 7 August 16:18
Subject: Re: I'm here!!

Stop that silly talk right now! You aren't dull at all. Or stupid. And I just know you can't be ugly, you're way too full of joie de vivre. You don't know for sure that Jamie was with Jessica today. Reading between the lines of your emails, I'd been getting the impression he wasn't all that keen on her. Why would he have done all those things with you on Saturday if she was the one he was sweet on? Why didn't he invite her to the woods with him? I have to be honest with you and say that at this moment in time I could quite happily choke Jessica on one of her vile crab sticks.

Your loyalty to your mum and sister are commendable, darling. In my weaker moments, like last night, I have to admit wishing that my own son was a little more devoted and hadn't gone swanning halfway around the world so soon after his father died. But I have to keep reminding myself that Dylan has his own life to live and his own way of dealing with the grief. You are entitled to have a life of your own, Georgie, and I'm sure your father would have wanted that too. Please tell me to mind my own business if I'm overstepping the mark. It just breaks my heart to think of you carrying so much responsibility upon your young shoulders. I wish there was some way I could help. Will send this now as I guess you must be waiting for my reply.

Nan xx

....

From: georgie*harris@hotmail.com
To: nancyblue#@aol.com
Date: Mon, 7 August 16:23
Subject: Re: I'm here!!

Are you OK? You must really miss having Dylan around. Does he email you a lot? I hope so. I know I've said it before but I don't know what I'd do if I didn't have you to email. I can't believe you thought I wouldn't bother emailing you any more! Even if I met the most amazing boy in the whole world – who didn't like girls like Jessica with their perfect blonde hair and stomachs that curve inwards – and he proposed to me and we eloped to somewhere really far away like America, and took my mum and Michaela with us – I would still always email you. I love our chats. Because it really feels like we're chatting, doesn't it? Even though I've never heard your voice! I don't think I've ever been able to talk to anyone the way I can talk to you, so you must never, ever think your silly thoughts either, OK! Just going to help Michaela find a book about Tigger and the heffalumps. Back soon.

G xx

From: nancyblue#@aol.com
To: georgie*harris@hotmail.com
Date: Mon, 7 August 16:29
Subject: Re: I'm here!!

Oh, now I'm crying again — but this time they're happy tears. Thank you so much for your kind words and I promise I won't be silly again. Dylan doesn't email too much. He hates computers, just like his dad. That's another reason I ended up dealing with all of his correspondence from fans. But he does phone me a couple of times a week to let me know how he's doing. It's silly, I really should take a leaf out of his book and just get on with things too, but it's so damned hard. Just when I think I'm making progress I get hit by a tidal wave of guilt and sorrow at getting on with life without Bruce. But I guess I need to take my own advice to you — it's what he would have wanted. I know because he told me just before he died. 'Don't ever lose your thirst for life, Nan,' he said. But it's so damned hard.

Let's make a deal, let's make sure that every day we do at least one thing for ourselves. Even if it's something tiny, like going for a walk or reading a favourite poem (none of my own compositions, I can assure you!) Do we have a deal?

Nan xx

PS: Have you ever talked to your mum about her getting professional help? Maybe she needs to see a counsellor?

....

From: georgie*harris@hotmail.com
To: nancyblue#@aol.com
Date: Mon, 7 August 16:39
Subject: Re: I'm here!!

I'm back! Michaela is talking to a friend of hers from nursery so I should get a few minutes peace! No, I don't bother talking to my mum about getting help because I know there's no point. The only time I ever tried she got really upset and accused me of interfering, so that was the end of that conversation! I like your idea about doing one thing for ourselves every day, and I promise I will really try. I guess still going to the drama workshop is me doing something for me, isn't it? Because I love singing and acting and this is the best part I have ever got. So I am NOT going to let the walking crab stick ruin that! Debbie was really nice to me in the rehearsal today. She said that if I – oh my God! Tone-Deaf!

From: nancyblue#@aol.com
To: georgie*harris@hotmail.com
Date: Mon, 7 August 16:42
Subject: Re: I'm here!!

Goodness Georgie, what's happened? I hope everything's OK? I'm going to leave my computer on. Email me as soon as you can to let me know you're all right.

Nan xx

....

From: nancyblue#@aol.com
To: georgie*harris@hotmail.com
Date: Mon, 7 August 23:34
Subject: Please email me!

Dear Georgie,
It's 11.30 p.m. and I just had a final check of my emails. I don't know why, the library must have shut hours ago, it's just that I've been really worried since your last email. Did your stepfather turn up in the library? How did he know you were there? Oh I do hope all is OK. You'll let me know what's happened as soon as you get the chance, won't you?

Don't worry, I will be checking my emails regularly from now on. My fog of gloom seems to have lifted a little. It's left me exhausted though, so I think I'll head off to bed. I'm going to venture back into my own room tonight. That sofa in Bruce's room has given me chronic backache! Sleep tight, Georgie, don't let the bed bugs bite! That's what I used to say to Dylan when he was little and I tucked him in at night.

Lots of love,
Nan xx

···

From: nancyblue#@aol.com
To: georgie*harris@hotmail.com
Date: Tue, 8 August 16:16
Subject: Where are you?

Dear Georgie,

Are you OK? I've been checking my emails all day but not a thing from you. It's 4.15 p.m. now so hopefully you'll be online at the library? Let me know . . .

Nan xx

From: nancyblue#@aol.com
To: georgie*harris@hotmail.com
Date: Wed, 9 August 02:34
Subject: Still worrying...

Oh Georgie, this is so frustrating. I keep telling myself that you're fine and you just haven't been able to get to a computer today. But the way you broke off in your last message, I can't help feeling that something terrible has happened. Why would Tone-Deaf show up at the library? If that is what happened . . .

I'm afraid I'm cursed with a ridiculously vivid imagination and right now, at 2.30 in the morning, it's going into overdrive. The weather isn't helping. I don't know what it's been like in London today but here in Hove it's been so humid. This afternoon, when I took Woodstock for his walk, the sky was a horrible yellowy grey, as if it was jaundiced, and the air was thick with the crackle of electricity. Poor Woodstock's tongue was trailing on the floor by the time we got back home, he was so thirsty. And the storm still hasn't broken.

I've been tossing and turning for hours, it's so damned hot. I did fall asleep briefly but had a horrible dream about Bruce. I used to like dreaming about him when he first died

181

because it was the next best thing to seeing him again. But not any more. Not the kind of dreams I keep having. Tonight I dreamt he was trapped in a sand dune and I was trying to pull him out, but all I had to pull him with was one of those children's fishing nets they sell at the seaside and it wasn't strong enough and he kept sinking further and further from reach. Hmm, doesn't take a genius to figure out what that was about does it? But what if I don't want to let go? What if I'd rather let him drag me under than let him go alone?

Oh, I'm sorry sweetie, I'm rambling off on a tangent again. Ooh, I think I just heard thunder! Going to go and watch from Bruce's window. There's nothing quite like watching a storm over the sea. Email me as SOON as you get the chance.

Lots of love,
Nan xx

From: nancyblue#@aol.com

To: georgie*harris@hotmail.com

Date: Wed, 9 August 16:59

Subject: Stormy weather

Another day and still no email. I don't know what to do because I don't want you to think I'm not concerned, so I guess I'll keep sending you messages in the hope that you can at least sense that I'm thinking of you – a bit like you did that time I emailed you about the sea.

The storm, when it finally came, was spectacular. I flung both windows in Bruce's study as wide as they would go and sat there on the ledge with his old cardigan around my shoulders, watching the elements battle it out. The sea was like a gigantic cauldron, bubbling and frothing away, and all I could do was watch in awe at the power of it all. And then something quite amazing happened, Georgie. I hope you don't mind me telling you this, but I feel I just have to tell someone, and you better than anyone else. Because last night it felt as if I had some kind of breakthrough. The jagged shard of grief that seemed to have wedged itself inside my heart finally came loose and fell away. And it was the storm that did it.

At first, as I watched the sky cracking open, I had no concern for my safety. In fact I felt quite exhilarated. I think a part of me was secretly hoping that the next lightning bolt would come crashing right down on me because then I could finally be reunited with Bruce. I kept picturing myself slipping through the crack in the sky to where he would be waiting for me on the other side. But then, as the storm continued to rage, something odd happened. I found myself looking back on my life and all I had done. The mistakes, the triumphs, the laughter, the tears. It was as if my entire life lay before me like a huge book, and do you know what I realised? I realised how bloody lucky I have been.

Even the lowest points, I saw looking back last night, were always followed by a high. Like learning I couldn't have kids (Dylan is adopted – you're not the only one who's been keeping a secret, darling). Somehow I made it through that terrible dark discovery and the years of angst that followed and was blessed with the perfect son. Every page of my life story that is home to a tragedy or regret has always been followed by a cause for joy. And in that moment, as the lightning flashed and the thunder roared, I realised that this time I am living through right now is just another page. And although it is inscribed with the most unbearable grief, it too will pass. So do you know what I did, Georgie? I took a deep breath and clenched my fists and in my mind I made myself turn over the page. It was so heart-wrenching and poignant but I knew I had to do it. I had to say goodbye to Bruce in order to move on.

Oh dear, I really have rambled this time, haven't I? But I wanted you to know what happened, Georgie, because I want you to see your life in the same way. Right now you are on a difficult page, but you won't be stuck here forever. You have so many pages yet to fill in your life story – all crisp and clean and full of promise. So whatever is happening right now, hold on to that thought and whenever you get the opportunity, have the courage to turn that page. Once again, I hope all is OK, darling, and please email me as soon as you can.

Lots of love,
Nan xx

....

From: georgie*harris@hotmail.com
To: nancyblue#@aol.com
Date: Thur, 10 August 19:09
Subject: Re: Stormy Weather

Tone-Deaf knows about the workshop. Jessica went round to my house on Monday and told him where I was. I don't know what she said – she probably pretended to be calling for me and then accidentally-on-purpose let it slip. I can just imagine her in her stupid fake accent going, 'Oh my gosh, I, like, totally forgot. She'll be at the drama workshop where she's been for, like, the past week, won't she?'

When Tone-Deaf turned up on Monday he went nuts. He shouted at me in front of everyone – in the library, where it's dead silent – so it sounded even worse. He called me a lying, deceitful little cow. And then he pulled me out by the arm. The librarian tried to stop him and Michaela started crying, but it didn't make any difference. All the way home he gripped on to the top of my arm with his huge hand. I've got a ring of purple bruises there now, like a horrible tattoo, he was holding on so tight. And he kept muttering stuff under his breath about how sick he was of me and my mum and how much he had done for us but this is all the thanks he gets. I don't think I've ever been as scared as I was on that walk home. I kept thinking, if he's doing this to me in public what is he going to do when we get indoors? I didn't cry though. Well, only a little bit, but I kept it silent and didn't let him see. He didn't touch me when we got home though. He didn't have to because he did something far worse. He told me something – about my dad. Something horrible. And now I feel as if my whole world has fallen apart. I'm really sorry, Nan, but I'm going to have to go.

I've been grounded so I shouldn't even be here at all, but Tone-Deaf is at work and I said to Angelica I had to pop out to see a friend and if she told him I would never, ever talk to her again for as long as I live. I hate her, Nan. I hate them both. Next week is the performance of Bugsy Malone but I will be stuck in my bedroom picturing Jamie and Jessica and all the others playing their roles while all of their loving mums and dads look on with tears in their eyes and big soppy grins on their faces. I feel as if my life is over before it's even had a chance to begin.

Thank you so much for your emails — I loved the one about the storm. I've got the librarian to print it out for me so I can read it properly in bed tonight. I really liked what you said about our lives being like books. What do you do though if you suddenly find out that whole chapters of your life could be lies? After what Tone-Deaf told me on Monday so many things I thought were real have been wiped out and rewritten by him.

I promise I'll email again as soon as I get the chance, but I'd better get back now, just in case he comes home early.

Lots of love,
Georgie xx

From: nancyblue#@aol.com
To: georgie*harris@hotmail.com
Date: Thur, 10 August 19:11
Subject: Re: Stormy weather

Georgie – are you still there? I want you to have my phone number and I want you to ring me as soon as you can – 01273 556 7840.

Lots of love,
Nan xx

....

From: nancyblue#@aol.com
To: georgie*harris@hotmail.com
Date: Thur, 10 August 23:08
Subject: Call me

Well, it's 11 p.m. and there's been no reply or call so I guess you must have gone home before you could get my phone number. Oh Georgie, I was horrified to receive your message, horrified.

Sometimes in life we need a little help 'turning the page'

and that's what I want to do for you now. I want you to call me as soon as you can and I want you to know that you do not have to stay in a house where you do not feel safe. I have been pacing up and down Bruce's study absolutely hopping mad at what has happened to you. How dare that man lay a finger on you! I keep wondering what Bruce would say about all of this. I know he would want me to do something. Bruce was a great one for doing, he found it physically impossible to sit back and witness injustice or cruelty of any kind. I know we've never met and I know I'm not a member of your family, but I am your friend, your true friend and I can't just sit here, staring at a computer screen while I know you are being treated in this way.

Please call me . . .
Nan xx

Part Four

Turning the Page

From: georgie*harris@hotmail.com
To: nancyblue#@aol.com
Date: Sat, 12th August 10:45
Subject: Re: Call me

Dear Nan,

It was so great to finally talk to you last night. You sounded just how I imagined – dead sophisticated and well spoken – like a proper actress, lol! (And I am laughing really loud as I am currently waiting for you in the internet café in Victoria Station and it is so noisy in here, what with all the tourists hustling and bustling about!!) I don't know why I'm emailing you when I'm about to meet you. Maybe it's because I'm so nervous.

It's been so easy to talk to you in emails, but what if it isn't the same face to face? What if once you see me you realise that I am just a stupid teenager with nothing interesting to say at all? The station announcer has just said that your train is running approximately 20 minutes late. So I suppose I'll carry on with this email for a while. It also gives me something to do – ever since I left home this morning I've felt like an escaped convict. Sitting here in the internet café typing away makes me feel a whole lot less conspicuous. Not that Angelica or Tone-Deaf have a clue where I am or anything, but still.

When I started to cry on the phone to you last night it wasn't because you upset me or anything. You were being so kind and your voice sounded so calm and strong, I couldn't help bursting into tears. And I'm sorry I couldn't bring myself to tell you what it was that Tone-Deaf said to me on Monday night. It's just so hard to even think about it right now, let alone say it out loud. Maybe I'm scared that if I *do* say it out loud it'll make it true and then I don't know what I'd do. I guess I'm still hoping Tone-Deaf and Angelica were lying. I can't believe she agreed with him, let him rewrite my history and hers, let him say those horrible things about Dad. This morning, when I told her I was going out I had to clench my fists really tightly in my pockets to stop myself from punching her. And I think she must have sensed it because she didn't argue, she just said, 'Make sure you get back before seven,' because of course that's when *he* will be back from the football and the pub.

I know what, I'll try writing down what happened, here, in this email, so that if I'm still not able to tell you when we meet I can just get you to go online and read it. I'll type it as a script because that's quickest. Here goes:

[SCENE: GEORGIE's *bedroom, Monday evening.* GEORGIE *is sitting on her bed, leaning against the wall, rubbing her bruised arm.* TONE-DEAF *is standing by the bedroom door, glaring.*]

TONE-DEAF: Look at you, nothing but a pathetic loser, just like your druggie dad and your pisshead mum.

GEORGIE: My dad didn't do drugs.

TONE-DEAF: [*laughing sarcastically*] Didn't do drugs? A long-haired roadie for the Magic Carpets? Of course he did drugs.

GEORGIE: You're lying!

TONE-DEAF: Oh yeah? How do you think he died then?

GEORGIE: He – he had an accident on his motorbike. The road was slippery from all the rain.

TONE-DEAF: [*snorting with laughter*] Yeah, right.

GEORGIE: [*starting to feel really sick*] What do you mean?

TONE-DEAF: He was off his head on God-knows-what and he got on his bike. That's how much your precious dad thought of you and your mum – and any other poor bugger he could have killed on the road.

GEORGIE: No!

TONE-DEAF: Yeah. But me? I put a roof over your head. I feed and clothe you – and what do I get in return? Nothing but lies.

GEORGIE: [*muttering*] You're the liar.

TONE-DEAF: [*stepping closer to her*] What?

GEORGIE: You – you're lying now. My dad didn't do drugs. You're lying.

TONE-DEAF: You ignorant little –

[*He is interrupted by the sound of* GEORGIE's *pathetic mum,* ANGELICA, *arriving home from work. She enters the room and sees* GEORGIE *crying on the bed.*]

ANGELICA: Oh my God? What's happened?

GEORGIE: He's lying, Mum, he's saying all this stuff about Dad and –

TONE-DEAF: This little cow is the one who's been lying to *us*.

ANGELICA: What do you mean? [*She looks at* GEORGIE] Lying about what?

GEORGIE: I haven't Mum, it's him, he –

TONE-DEAF: She's been going to that drama workshop, up at the community centre. The one we said she couldn't go to. She was there all last week – when she was supposed to be looking after my daughter.

[*He takes a step closer to the bed,* GEORGIE *hugs her teddy bear.*]

ANGELICA: What? But –

TONE-DEAF: She just left poor little Michaela all on her own so she could ponce around pretending to be an actress.

GEORGIE: I didn't leave her on her own, she was with me all the time, she –

ANGELICA: Georgie, how could you? I told you not —

TONE-DEAF: Oh yeah, you told her not to go. And since when has she ever listened to a word you say? She's her father's daughter all right.

GEORGIE: Mum, he said that Dad was on drugs. He wasn't, was he? He said he was on drugs the night he died. He said that's why he died. Mum?

[ANGELICA *stares blankly at the floor, clasping and unclasping her hands.*]

TONE-DEAF: Go on — tell her. Tell her the state he was in that night. Tell her how you begged him not to go out like that. Tell her what her precious dad was really like.

GEORGIE: Mum!

[ANGELICA *nods her head really slowly, still not looking up.*]

GEORGIE: [*screaming*] Get out!

[TONE-DEAF *starts to grin and leaves the room. ANGELICA takes a step towards the bed. GEORGIE flings Hendrix, her teddy bear, at her. The teddy bear bought for her by her 'druggie' dad.*]

GEORGIE: Get out!

[ANGELICA *leaves the room.*]

So now you can see why I didn't want to tell you what happened. How can she have lied to me for all those years and told me he died in a tragic accident when all along it was his own fault? All along he was a —

Maybe she wasn't lying though. Maybe she was just too scared of Tone-Deaf to stand up to his lies? I don't know what to think and I keep trying to replay the memories I have left of my dad, looking for something – anything – that will tell me the truth. But I can't find a thing. All I can remember are blurry little glimpses, like I'm peering at him through a net curtain. His smile, his twinkling eyes, the way he would throw his head back when he laughed. But if he was what Tone-Deaf says, and if that is the real reason he died, what did he think of me? And my mum? To get on his bike in that kind of state. Not caring if he lived or died.

Oh my God! They're announcing your train's arrival. This feels so strange, finishing an email to you so that I can actually go and meet you! I hope you like me!

Lots of love,
Georgie xx

....

Dearest Georgie,

Well darling, you would be extremely proud of me if you could see me now – tapping away among the trendy young things at the Victoria Station internet café. I had some time to kill before my train back to Brighton so I thought I'd send you a quick message. I wanted to tell you I had the nicest time today. It was completely and utterly frost-free to finally meet you, darling. You were everything I was expecting and more. So funny and smart and really quite beautiful.

I've just read the email you sent me while you were waiting for me here earlier and it made me shudder to go through it all again. I'm so glad you found the courage to tell me what happened when we met, and I hope the advice I gave you helped. As I said to you, we all make our own truths. Tone-Deaf can try and distort yours but you don't have to let him. Even if your father did take drugs it doesn't make him a bad person. Tone-Deaf wants you to think this because it makes him feel better. He is a typical, insecure bully. The way you remember your dad is the way he was – funny and charming and loving. Don't let Tone-Deaf rewrite your memories of him, they are way too precious – they are part of who you are.

I didn't tell Dylan he was adopted until he was fifteen. Bruce thought we should have told him a lot earlier but I just couldn't bring myself to. I guess I wanted to pretend he really was all mine. I didn't want him knowing someone else gave birth to him. I was terrified he might want to track her down and end up loving her more than me. In the end, as with all of my pig-headed decisions, it turned around and bit me on the backside. He was so upset and angry with me for not telling him sooner and I remember he went through a phase like you are now of questioning his identity. But you are who you decide to be, don't you see? Regardless of what your stepfather says, you can be whoever you want. Remember that, Georgie, and stay strong.

Did you enjoy your tour of London's theatreland? I hope you don't think it was terribly self-indulgent of me, taking you to all of my former haunts, but I wanted to give you something to aspire to. So you can dream of one day having your name in lights too. Oh Georgie, I got so much from today, I can't begin to tell you. It was so nice to be reminded of how my life used to be, and although I know it will never be the same without Bruce by my side, I still have possibilities, I still have hope. Good luck tonight. I hope your mum finds the leaflets I gave you useful and your talk with her goes well. I'm going to dust off my copy of Macbeth when I get home and have a go at reading some of my old speeches. I wonder if I still know any of them by heart?

Thank you again, and remember to call me if you need anything, anything at all, and at any time, day or night.

Lots of love,
Nan xx

....

From: georgie*harris@hotmail.com
To: nancyblue#@aol.com
Date: Sat, 12th August 18:47
Subject: Re: Thank you

Hi Nan,

That's so funny – I had to email you too! I've stopped off at the internet café on Ruislip High Street on my way home. It's nearly 7 p.m. but I don't know when I'll be able to get to a computer again and I wanted you to know I had THE BEST TIME today. Of course I didn't mind going around all of the theatres. I can't believe you've acted in so many of them! It seems impossible to believe that the name Georgie Harris could ever be twinkling down upon Shaftsbury Avenue or Drury Lane but it is a really lovely dream. To be honest, a few months ago, I used to dream of my name alongside Dylan's in the Jessop Close credits, but that seems really weird now. It's funny isn't it, how normally you don't notice yourself growing up, but every now and again it happens so fast it's like watching one of those sped-up films of a flower growing and you cringe at how babyish you used to be.

Thank you so much for the delicious lunch. Neal's Yard is so cool! I didn't know places like that still existed. It was like being in an Austin Powers movie – I hope you noticed I didn't say the olden days! I'm going to ask Angelica if I can make a carrot cake one day when Tone-Deaf is out. I had no idea carrots could taste so good! Thank you for the scented candle and the rose quartz crystal. That Laughing Buddha shop was amazing wasn't it? It reminded me of Aladdin's cave, crammed full of beautiful-smelling treasure! I'm going to keep the crystal in my pocket at all times so I can hold it whenever I need to and feel strong. It's so cool you can get different coloured crystals for every mood and emotion, isn't it? When I get some money from somewhere I am going to get you a piece of jade. That was the one for friendship and luck by the way.

I'm really pleased you are going to look at your Macbeth script. Do you think you would ever go back into acting? You know when we were standing outside the Theatre Royal? Well, I couldn't help looking at your face and you looked just like Michaela does when she's gazing into the window of the toyshop. You looked so excited and I could tell about a million magical memories were whizzing before your eyes like shooting stars. I bet Bruce would have wanted you to start acting again too.

Oh well, better get home before the psycho gets back. You're right, I mustn't let him ruin my memories of Dad. I feel so much happier now. I just know once I've talked to Mum and shown her those leaflets you gave me I'll make her see sense. You never know, maybe next time I email you we will have left home and be free of that nasty bully forever!

Lots of love,
Georgie xxx

....

From: nancyblue#@aol.com
To: georgie*harris@hotmail.com
Date: Sun, 13th August 10:18
Subject: New beginnings . . .

Dearest Georgie,

I just had to email you to tell you what happened last night. After I had picked Woodstock up from Ricardo's – and got drenched in sloppy kisses (from Woodstock not Ricardo!) I came back home and ransacked my loft. When Bruce and I adopted Dylan I packed all of my acting memorabilia away. I think I was hoping it would be a case of out of sight out of mind. After losing all hope of ever having kids I felt I'd suddenly been given this amazing chance at motherhood and I didn't want to blow it. I didn't want anything to get in the way. So, like callously discarding a lover, I packed all of my old scripts and programmes and props and costumes into a large trunk in the attic. And they've been up there gathering dust ever since. But, after my wander along memory lane yesterday, I couldn't resist bringing the trunk down from the attic and I spent half of last night trawling through it.

It was incredible, the emotions it unleashed. A bit like Pandora's Box, but without the serpent hair or deadly diseases I hasten to add! I even tried on several of the costumes. And they still fit!!! Then I read through the scrapbooks containing my old reviews and it was like being reintroduced to who I used to be and what I was (and maybe still am) capable of. It was such a distant chapter in my life I had forgotten all about the extraordinary sense of accomplishment I got from acting. When you become a wife and mother it's so easy to lose sight of the person you are at heart. At the time I really didn't mind – I was so happy being a wife to Bruce and a mum to Dylan. But who was I being to me?

Oh this probably doesn't make any sense to you, but what I am trying to say, what I've just figured out, is that my life isn't over. I'm still the same person The Times theatre reviews described as 'a luminescent presence'. I'm still the woman who 'made Lady Macbeth her own' and 'commanded the stage'. What was I thinking, going to poetry classes? It was like I was looking for myself in all the wrong places. The real me was right under my nose (or up in my attic) all along!

Let me give you a piece of advice, Georgie, and I want you to swear to me that you will always remember it. Never, ever lose sight of who you really are. Not in the face of bullying stepdads or even loving husbands or sons. Always keep hold of the real you. Always have that secret garden inside of yourself to escape to.

I hope everything was OK when you got home last night and if you gave those leaflets to your mum I hope they helped. It is so easy for a woman to feel trapped in a marriage, but she really doesn't have to stay with that horrible man if she doesn't want to. Refuge are a fantastic organisation, they have plenty of safe houses for women and their kids to go to. Promise me, Georgie, you'll ring or email me with any news. I'm keeping everything crossed for you (apart from my eyes obviously – that's really not a good look).

Going to take Woodstock for a stroll along the beach now – all of a sudden I have so much to think about.

Lots of love,
Nan xx

....

From: georgie*harris@hotmail.com
To: nancyblue#@aol.com
Date: Sun, 13th August 11:18
Subject: Re: New beginnings . . .

I hate my mum! I hate her! She is a selfish, ungrateful, ignorant cow and I wish she was dead! OK, I don't really mean that last bit, but she might as well be dead, the way she treats life as if it's just something that can be wasted. But the thing about life is you can't trade it in for a new one and you never know when your time is going to be up. Look at what happened to my dad and Bruce. But my mum just keeps on going through the motions, miserable and unhappy, as if she knows she's going to get another, much better chance at life one day. But what if she doesn't? And it's not just her life she's ruining either.

I gave her the leaflets. Last night, when I got back home. Tone-Deaf had called to say he was going out with his mates and wouldn't be back till this morning, so I thought it was the perfect opportunity. I thought she would be so fed up with him she would jump at the chance of escaping. But she went nuts. She told me I had no right telling her what to do and that I was just a child and I didn't understand. So then I told her about you. I didn't mean to, but she had made me so mad I wanted her to know that there was an adult who thought she ought to leave Tone-Deaf too. I wish I hadn't told her though because it made things a million times worse.

First of all I said 'an adult friend of mine' thought she ought to leave him and that was who had got the leaflets for her. I knew as soon as I said it I'd made a big mistake. 'What adult friend?' she asked, whilst pouring herself a vodka and not even bothering to hide it like she usually does in a glass of Coke. I thought about telling her all about Dylan and the website and how I'd thought I was emailing him but really it was you, but that wasn't a bad thing at all because I'd ended up making the best friend I've ever had. But then I realised it would only make things even more complicated, so I just said, 'one of my friend's mums.' She went quiet after that and took a large swig of her drink. For a split second I thought maybe she was having second thoughts, maybe she'd hug me and say how sorry she was and how I was right and yes, she would ring the people at Refuge straight away. But I was very wrong. 'You have no right discussing my personal business with your friends and their mums,' she hissed at me and the tips of her pale cheeks flushed an angry red. 'Tony is my husband and I know he can be a little —' She stopped and looked around the room (obviously trying to find a nice way to say obnoxious psycho bully). 'I know he can be a little difficult at times, but I love him.' I've never heard the word love said in such a flat, lifeless way. And I didn't believe her for a second. 'How can you?' I shouted. 'How can you love him, he's nothing but a selfish bully. What about the way he treats me? Don't you care about that?' The weird thing is, she actually looked shocked when I said it. Her big, grey, lifeless eyes actually widened and her mouth dropped open. 'What do you mean?' she said.

Well, that was it. I started yelling and I couldn't stop. All the stuff I've been bottling up, all the things I've been emailing you instead of telling her came tumbling out. About how badly I want to be an actress and how pleased I was to finally get a decent part and how much I had been loving the drama workshop but all the time completely terrified that I would be found out, and that Tone-Deaf would do something to me, smash me up the way he had done the shower. And how he'd bruised my arm the day he did find out and the thing that had hurt the most – the horrible things he'd said about Dad. And how she'd just hovered around in the background all the time like a frightened little shadow. 'You're supposed to be my mum,' I finished, 'you're supposed to look after me and protect me, but you're always too busy looking after yourself.' And then I ran up to my room and flung myself on my bed and cried and cried and waited for her footsteps to come creaking across the landing and for the bed to sink down as she sat on the edge of it and for her to stroke my hair the way she used to do and tell me everything was going to be all right. But she never came. Instead I just heard the clink of the vodka bottle against her glass and the low murmur of the television droning on into the night.

I don't know what I'm going to do, Nan. I feel as if the few nice things I had in my life have been taken away one by one. Jamie, the drama workshop, my so-called friends. And now I feel as if I have no one — apart from you. I'm sorry this email is so miserable, especially as yours was full of good news. And I am really happy you have found your old self again. And really excited that you might go back into acting. Better get back now.

Lots of love,
Georgie xx

....

From: nancyblue#@aol.com
To: georgie*harris@hotmail.com
Date: Sun, 13th August 16:12
Subject: Sorry – again!

Oh no! Oh Georgie, I'm so sorry. I feel as if every time I try to help you I end up making things a million times worse. But perhaps things aren't quite as bad as you think. Sometimes, when we hear the things we really don't want to hear, they take a little time to come to terms with. Your mum needed to hear all the things you said to her, even if it seemed as if she didn't. At least now she knows how you truly feel. At least now she has no excuses. It's as if you've planted a seed and now you have to sit back and wait and see what it might grow into. Give her time. And stay strong. Don't forget, I'm only a phone call away if you need me.

All my love,
Nan xx

....

From: georgie*harris@hotmail.com
To: nancyblue#@aol.com
Date: Mon, 14 August 16:59
Subject: Miracles

You were right!!! I planted a seed and it grew into a miracle!

All day yesterday there was a really weird atmosphere at home, as if the stormy weather had snuck in through the windows and under the doors and was waiting to break right over our heads. Everything was too quiet, too calm. When Tone-Deaf came rolling in – at ten past one in the afternoon, reeking of stale cigarettes and perfume and beer – Angelica just smiled at him sweetly and asked him how his night had been. But there was something about her smile, something about the way it stopped dead at her lips and never made it to her eyes that told me something was really wrong. Normally when Tone-Deaf has been out all night she'll cry or ask questions or sulk, but not this time. And I think he knew something was up too, because he was extra nice to her, telling her to go and put her feet up while he got the dinner ready. But Angelica shook her head really firmly and then she said, 'Why don't you have a rest? I bet you could do with some sleep.' Normally if she'd said something like that I would have shaken my head and tutted as soon as he left he room, but not this time. Because

212

although what she said was pathetic and sappy, the way she said it was strong as steel. As if what she was really saying was, 'I hate you, you bastard.' He knew it too, because he didn't go and lie down, he just kept hovering around trying to find ways to help her or be nice to her and every time she would answer him in the same steely way, until finally he went and sat on the couch and hid behind the sports section of the Sunday paper. She was really weird with me too, telling me to do things like pick up Michaela's colouring pencils or check on the roast potatoes but not really looking at me at all.

As soon as we'd had lunch I disappeared up to my bedroom. All the way through the meal the storm clouds had been building and I really didn't want to be there when they burst. I had almost drifted off into a doze when I heard the kitchen door slamming. I crept out on to the landing to try and hear what was happening but the noise from the football on the TV kept drowning it out. All I heard were random shouted words. 'Understand' and 'enough' from my mum and 'trying' and 'for God's sake' from him. Then it all went quiet again. I went back to my room, I heard Tone-Deaf go and have a shower and then go to bed. I didn't go downstairs for about an hour after that. My stomach was a churning mixture of roast dinner and dread. I had been expecting to find my mum with one of her glasses of 'Coke', slumped on the sofa and crying. But she wasn't, she was making a jigsaw puzzle with Michaela and talking and laughing as if nothing had happened. It was so weird. But it's what happened this morning that was the real miracle.

At about 8 o'clock Angelica came into my bedroom and woke me up. She wasn't wearing her work uniform and had actually put on some make-up. You should see her when she wears make-up, she looks even more beautiful, even more like a china doll. 'Get up,' she whispered. Michaela was still asleep in her bed across from me. I had been in the middle of a nightmare about singing on stage at a talent contest but every time I opened my mouth a jet of vegetable oil came spurting out. 'What's happened?' I asked, rubbing my eyes. 'Nothing's happened,' she replied, 'you just need to get up.' I frowned at her. 'Why?' She stared down at me through her thick, dark lashes. 'So you can get to your drama workshop on time.'

Well, you can imagine how shocked I was. I had to kick my legs together under the duvet to make sure I wasn't still dreaming. 'What?' was all I could manage to say, but by then Angelica had stood up and was opening my wardrobe. She turned and looked down at me, smiling that same funny smile from yesterday, the one that didn't quite reach her eyes. 'You still want to go, don't you?' she asked. I nodded, too shocked to be able to actually say anything. It was only later, when I was wolfing down some toast in the kitchen that I dared to ask about Tone-Deaf. 'What about him?' Angelica replied, not turning from the sink where she was rinsing out her coffee mug. 'He said I couldn't go. He said I have to look after Michaela.' Still she didn't turn round. But she did answer me. 'Well, *I* said you can go. And you're *my* daughter.' Oh Nan, when she said that I wanted to run over and give her a massive hug, but there was something about the way she was standing that told me not to. Like she had 'KEEP AWAY' written in red capitals across her stiff back. 'Go on then, you don't want to be late,' she said, finally turning round. 'And don't worry about Michaela, I'm taking the week off work so I can look after her.'

All the way down our road I wanted to sing for joy – until I saw Tone-Deaf's cab pulling into the Close. My stomach looped the loop as I watched him approach but rather than stop and ask me where the hell I was going he just sped up and roared off towards home. I hope he wasn't horrible to Mum. Maybe that's what they were arguing about yesterday? Maybe Mum told him I had to be allowed to go to the workshop? It feels weird thinking she might have actually stood up to him for once.

I was dead scared when I got to the community centre. I thought Debbie would be really mad at me for not showing up most of last week. Luckily I got there before any of the others, so I had the chance to talk to her in private. I told her my step-nan had been really ill after nearly choking to death on a toffee and Debbie gave me a hug and said I shouldn't worry because quite a few people had been off with holidays and stuff and if I thought I could get all my lines learnt by Wednesday I could still play Blousey because no one else was able to do the part as well as me! And Nan, you are not going to believe my next piece of news – Jessica and Kate One have left the group for good. I was absolutely dreading seeing them but Kate Two said they didn't come at all last week and won't be coming back. Apparently Jessica told Kate Two that Bugsy Malone was too immature for her and she was sick of hanging out with kids. From the way Kate rolled her eyes when she told me I got the feeling that she's pretty sick of Jessica too. Jamie wasn't there either so I assumed he must have left to hang out with Jessica. This tall thin boy called Peter was playing Bugsy instead and it wasn't the same at all. When he kissed his finger and touched my nose I didn't get the slightest flutter in my tummy. In fact I felt sick because his finger was all slimy with spit. And although I'd got what I wanted and I was back in the show, I couldn't help feeling a bit empty inside. Nothing was the same now, and what if

Tone-Deaf was making Mum's life a misery just so I could be there?

It wasn't until the very end of the day that things began to get a whole lot better. I was trudging out of the community centre wondering whether I'd done the right thing by coming back, when I heard someone call out, 'Hey, Blousey.' And it was him. Jamie. I spun around and saw him sitting under the willow tree by the duck pond. I think I must have just stood there open-mouthed for a while because then he shouted, 'Well? Are you coming over or what?'

Have you ever felt overjoyed, terrified and sick all in one go? Because that is exactly how I felt as I slowly walked over. I tried to look cool but unfortunately my mouth kept curling into a silly grin, no matter how hard I bit on my lip. 'So, what's up?' he said as I reached him and stood there scuffing my foot on the dried grass. 'Sit down?' he said, but like a question rather than an order and in his softest gruff voice. So I dropped my bag and sat down next to him and stared out to the pond, where a couple of ducks were gliding slowly towards the reeds in the middle. 'All right?' I think I said. 'Yep,' I think he replied. And then I looked at him and he was staring at me, his long fringe parted on either side of his eyes, like a pair of dark silk curtains and he looked so worried it made me want to cry. 'You OK?' he asked and I nodded. 'I'm sorry about what happened last Saturday – in the woods,' I said slowly. 'I'm sorry I messed everything up.' He gave this short, angry little laugh and said, 'You didn't mess anything up. It was that stupid, stuck-up mate of yours.' I gulped and looked at him. 'What do you mean?'

I'd spent all week imagining him and Jessica getting it together, so what he was saying didn't make any sense. 'The way she turned up like that,' he replied. 'The things she said to you, about your mum and that.' My cheeks were hot and I turned away. 'I didn't invite her you know. She must have followed us.' Jamie nodded. 'I know.' Then he lay down on his side, looking up at me. 'What did you go and run off for?' he asked. 'I came after you. Why didn't you wait for me?'

It was so weird. Everything I thought had happened, everything I'd been putting together in my mind like a jigsaw, suddenly started to fall apart before my eyes. Jessica and Jamie holding hands by the fire. Jessica going round to Jamie's house for crab-stick sandwiches. Jessica snogging Jamie's face off. And then, in their place, a much nicer jigsaw of thoughts started to form. Jamie coming after me in the woods. Jamie caring about me. Jamie thinking Jessica was stupid and stuck-up.

'I was embarrassed,' I muttered and I could feel my cheeks going an even darker shade of red. I glanced down out of the corner of my eye and saw that Jamie was nodding. 'She's a spiteful little cow,' he said quietly. 'And I told her so after you'd gone.' I turned and looked straight at him. 'What?'

'I told her,' he said, 'exactly what I thought of her. I'd been wanting to do it for ages. She's been driving me mental always hanging around, so full of herself. I only ever talked to her because she was your mate.' WHAT?!!! Now completely random jigsaw thoughts were flying into my head. Jamie only talked to Jessica because she was MY mate. He thought she was a spiteful little cow. Jamie hated Jessica — and he liked me!

'So what's the story with your mum then?' he asked. And his voice was so soft and his eyes were so full of concern I really didn't want to lie to him. But I didn't want to tell him the whole truth either. So I told him how my mum had found it hard to cope ever since Dad had died and some-times she would get drunk, but not very often and really everything was fine and I had got upset because I was so embarrassed by what Jessica had said — lying about me inviting her to the woods and saying that stuff about my mum. I talked on and on and then, when I finally came to a stop, Jamie sat up and then he kissed his finger and touched my nose, just like he had to do in the show. Only this time it wasn't the show and we weren't even rehearsing.

'So, you back at the workshop for good?' he asked. I nodded and he said, 'Great, I'll see you there tomorrow then.' And all I could think was that this kind of thing doesn't happen to me, only in my dreams and even then it isn't half as amazing. Then Jamie stood up and held his hand out to me and we walked all the way up the high street hand in hand, not saying a word, just looking at each other every now and again and smiling. When we got to the bus station he said he had to go because he was supposed to be helping his dad strip a bike and had told him he was only popping out for a pint of milk. I nodded and then he said again that he'd see me tomorrow at the workshop and I said 'OK' and then his bus drew up and he started to get on it but then he turned and jumped back down and gave me a massive hug. It was really lovely, until the driver shouted out, 'Come on, sonny, I've got a timetable to keep!'

I've come straight to the library, my hand still tingling from where he was holding it, because I had to tell you what happened before I go home. Oh Nan, surely as you get older your life should become more straightforward? But for me it just seems to be getting more and more weird.

Exactly one week ago I was sitting here, at this very table with all the dried bubblegum underneath, thinking my world had come to an end. Tone-Deaf had told me that stuff about my dad and I felt certain Jamie hated me and would never speak to me again. Now I'm free and back at the workshop and Jamie hates Jessica and I think he likes me!! How weird is that?! There was a moment, when he was hugging me at the bus station, when I thought that he might even actually kiss me. Properly. Not just kissing his finger and touching my face. I've never been kissed by a boy before. I always thought it would be dead scary, but when I'm with Jamie I feel so safe.

Oh my God, Nan, my entire body is fizzing with excitement. I don't care what the atmosphere is like at home between mum and Tone-Deaf tonight, nothing is going to ruin my happy mood.

Lots and lots of love,
Georgie xxx

....

From: nancyblue#@aol.com
To: georgie*harris@hotmail.com
Date: Mon, 14 August 21:22
Subject: Re: Miracles

I told you!!! I knew he liked you and not the walking crab stick! Oh darling, this is so exciting! (Something tells me I will be using a lot of exclamation marks in this email!!!) I am so, so pleased that something nice has happened to you after everything else that's gone on lately. Moments like this are what life is all about, Georgie, they are the threads of gold that illuminate the rest of the tapestry.

I do hope everything was OK when you returned home this evening? It certainly sounds as if the seed you planted has taken root. I wanted to shout 'Atta girl!' when I heard about your mum. Maybe now she will start to find the courage to stand up to your stepfather once and for all. The cheek of the man, staying out all night and coming home reeking of perfume! If Bruce had ever done anything like that to me I would have had his private parts for garters!

Anyway, back to matters of a more heart-warming nature. It sounds to me as if a kiss between you and your leading man might not be all that far off, so you'd better be prepared. Would you like some advice? Next time you're beneath your willow tree or having a heart-to-heart and you want him to know that you want to be kissed, try the following techniques:

Lick your lips, slowly and languorously.
Whilst talking to him let your eyes flit from each of his eyes to his mouth and back again – this is known as the triangular gaze or passion pyramid due to the eyes and mouth forming a triangular shape.
Look at him through lowered lashes with your head slightly bowed – the late, tragic Princess Diana was a master at this one!
Giggle a lot, but NOT manically or hysterically – it's not in the least bit seductive!

Ooh, this is so much fun – do let me know THE MINUTE anything happens, won't you? Am off to bed now, to dream of my first kiss with Bruce, backstage at the Old Vic on opening night. Wishing you sweet dreams of Jamie . . .

All my love,
Nan xx

....

From: georgie*harris@hotmail.com
To: nancyblue#@aol.com
Date: Tue, 15 August 17:35
Subject: Rehearsing!

Hi Nan,

Am at Jamie's house, on his mum's computer – we have come here to 'rehearse' – rofl (rolling on floor laughing!!)

All OK at home – the dreaded TD has been out all the time so things nice and relaxed – Mum still a bit weird with me, but at least she's letting me go out. Got to go now – Jamie's going to play me a new song he's written. Hope all is ok with you?

Lots of love,
Georgie xx

From: nancyblue#@aol.com
To: georgie*harris@hotmail.com
Date: Tue, 15 August 19:01
Subject: Re: Rehearsing!

Dearest Georgie,

'Rehearsing', huh? I have a feeling that your scenes together are going to be the most rehearsed in history!

Well, darling, you aren't the only one who's been having fun, I am glad to report. Today I actually plucked up the courage to look up my old agent, Laurence Bingham, or Bing as he's known in the business. To be honest I had a horrible feeling he might have snuffed it by now – he seemed about 80 when I first joined him and that was, well, it was quite some time ago. But he's still there, in his Georgian townhouse off the Charing Cross Road. Still chewing on his stubby cigar no doubt, as he fondles his velvet bow tie and calls everyone 'Aaaaaaaaaaangel'. It took me about five attempts to dial his number. I kept slamming the receiver down before I'd even got to the end of the London dialling code, but after a brisk walk to the beach with Woodstock and giving myself a sharp telling off en route – I made the paper boy jump out of his skin, poor darling, when I rounded the corner to my house shouting to myself, 'For God's sake, have you no gumption?!' The poor boy looked into his bag all flustered and replied, 'Sorry, Miss, the Guardians have all gone.' Anyway, after that I marched around my living room shouting, 'I AM FABULOUS' several hundred times – I highly recommend it for when you are feeling at your weakest, darling, works a treat – and then I grabbed the phone and dialled the entire number AND managed to hang on long enough for it to be picked up. When the receptionist asked for my name I fought the overwhelming urge to say Dame Judi Dench and then waited in agony as I was put on hold.

Why do they always play such dreary music while you're on hold? I suppose it is to keep you calm while you wait, but listening to Greensleeves on loop really did nothing for my nerves, I can tell you! I kept picturing Bing sat behind his huge desk, furrowing his brow as he strained to remember who I was or, even worse, remembering, and making up an excuse to get rid of me. I really wasn't prepared at all for his voice to actually come on the line. But it did!! 'Nancy, my aaaaaaaaangel!' he bellowed, nearly sending my receiver flying. 'How the devil are you, old girl?' I decided to ignore the 'old'. It turns out that not only does he remember me, but he has been following Dylan's career with interest and – get this – hoping against hope I would one day decide to make a return to the boards!

Oh Georgie, darling, I am so excited. I'm meeting him tomorrow at a restaurant in Charlotte Street and he's already talking about putting me up for some parts. I'm not sure if I'm quite ready for that yet though rofsmh (rolling on floor shaking my head!). It feels as if my life is imitating yours. One minute it felt as if everything was over, the next minute everything's hurtling forwards again at full pelt. Maybe this is what happens when you vow to turn the page? Maybe the Universe has been sitting there, patiently keeping everything on hold, so that the minute we decided to get on with our lives everything fell neatly into place. Either way, I am so excited – for both of us.

Do keep me up to date with your 'rehearsals' won't you, even if it's just a brief message, and I will of course let you know how my lunch goes tomorrow.

Lots of love,
Nan xx

....

From: georgie*harris@hotmail.com
To: nancyblue#@aol.com
Date: Wed, 16 August 16:32
Subject: Latest update . . .

Hi Nan,

What exciting news!! I hope your meeting went well. I'm trying to imagine what you wore — something dead glamorous I bet. I loved that dress you were wearing the day we met, you looked so sophisticated and that shade of green really suits you.

Right now I'm in the library doing an internet search for my dad. Don't worry, I haven't gone radio rental, as Jamie would say. (It's cockney rhyming slang for mental but don't ask me why!!) I haven't forgotten my dad is dead, I guess I'm looking for clues. Despite Angelica letting me go to the drama workshop she still won't talk to me properly. Last night I tried again, while she was cleaning out the fridge. 'Was Dad really on drugs?' I asked from the kitchen doorway. Her body went all rigid against the white light. 'I don't want to talk about it,' was all she would say. And the thing is, if Dad wasn't, if what Tone-Deaf had said was a lie, then she would have told me so, wouldn't she? Because Tone-Deaf wasn't there last night, so she didn't have anything to be scared of, or any reason to lie. But she wouldn't say any more and I didn't want to push it because I didn't want to give her a reason to get drunk – she hasn't had a drink since Saturday night.

So I've come down here to the library after the workshop to see if there's anything I can find and I'm going to trawl through all 3,700,000 search results for Jeff Harris. Obviously it might take me more than one visit! Why oh why couldn't my dad have been called something exotic and unusual like Pendragon Vanderbilt or Joshua Ironingboardhead? It would have been so much easier to find him! Of course when I do a search for 'Jeff Harris Magic Carpets' I get a couple of results. One's on the Magic Carpets' website, where they have a memorial to him, and there's another mention on a fan site where they talk about how the song 'Too Young' was inspired by his death. I found the song on YouTube and it's really lovely. All about how full of life my dad was, but there's no mention of drugs. Not that I want there to be, but I guess I'd rather find out the truth for myself than give Tone-Deaf the satisfaction of rewriting my life.

That's the worst thing about all this. Before it happened, my dad was mine. Tone-Deaf and Angelica and Michaela all had each other but at least I had Dad to myself, even if he was dead. But now it feels as if Tone-Deaf has taken that too. Taken all I had left of Dad and replaced him with someone horrible and selfish. I need to know that what he said wasn't true. That my dad *was* nice and caring and funny and loving, just the way I remember him.

I wanted to tell Jamie about it today at the workshop. Now Michaela doesn't have to come with me I can go outside at lunchtime, and today we headed straight for the willow tree. I could see Kate Two and some of the other girls watching us and I felt amazing. I don't think they could quite believe I was sitting on my own with Jamie. I don't think I could believe it either. And I know this probably sounds really petty and childish but I hope someone rings Jessica tonight and tells her and I hope she cries until she is sick all over her stupid pink bed and its stupid heart-shaped cushions! But anyway, when it came down to it I just couldn't tell Jamie about my dad, so we talked about music and which flavour Fruit Pastille we like best instead. I did try your techniques for getting him to kiss me, but when I did that passion pyramid thing and looked at his mouth he said, 'Have I got ketchup on my lip or something?' (He had had a hotdog for lunch.) And then, when I tried to look at him through lowered eye lashes he said, 'What's wrong with your neck?'

How low are you supposed to tilt your head by the way? I think I might have overdone it. But I'm not all that bothered because all I can think about is my dad.

You know when we met up in London and you told me that story about Dylan and how when he first found out he had been adopted he ran out of the house and you found him down in that cove throwing pebbles into the sea? Well I think I understand why he did that. When someone tells you your parents aren't who you thought they were, it changes who you think you are too. I know it shouldn't and I know you said we are who we decide to be, but isn't that decision also based on the people who physically made us? Until I know who my dad really was I can't be certain of my own identity, and while I can't be certain of that I can't even think about Jamie and me.

Oh my God, I can't believe I just typed that!! You know those surveys where they work out how much of your life you spend asleep or eating or on the toilet or whatever and it works out to be months or even years? Well I reckon I must have spent about five years of my life wondering if any boy would ever like me enough to kiss me or ask me out and now I'm saying that Jamie Phelps will have to wait!! Ho-hum, back to the search I guess. Did you know there is someone called Jeff Harris in Texas who is the owner of the world's oldest mouth organ?!!

Let me know how your lunch went.

Lots of love,
Georgie xx

....

From: nancyblue#@aol.com
To: georgie*harris@hotmail.com
Date: Wed, 16 August 21:42
Subject: Re: Latest update . . .

Hi Darling,

Just a thought, but is there no one you could go and see about your dad? Somebody who knew him really well – a friend perhaps or a member of the Flying Carpets or whatever they were called? Did he have any brothers or sisters? What about his parents, your grandparents? I seem to remember you saying that you weren't allowed to see them any more, but would it not be possible to phone them at least? I don't like the idea of you having to trawl through

3 million websites; the words needle and world's largest haystack spring to mind. However, never one to shirk from a challenge, I shall put in a couple of hours searching myself tonight and see what I come up with.

My lunch was divine. Bing is about 100 years old but still a terrible gossip and so funny. I now know who just about everyone in the acting world is sleeping with and who stabbed who in the back for which part. It was all excellent fun, even the bit where Bing reprimanded our waitress for forgetting my starter. 'Don't you know who this is?' he demanded, so loud the entire restaurant turned around. 'This is Nancy Martin.' About a month ago I would have winced to hear my maiden name. I would have probably leapt up and said, 'No, no, I'm Nancy Curtland,' and fled in tears. But not today. Today I just nodded and smiled.

You are Georgie Harris, darling, and you need to do whatever it takes to find out what that means. Thank you for what you said about Dylan, this is really helping me understand what he went through. He never bothered tracking down his real parents in the end. But it was different for him because he'd never known them. When he finally forgave me for keeping it from him he told me he didn't want to know who they were because he was happy with the parents he already had. But as I said, it was completely different for him. I'm off to do some searching for you now, let me know how you get on.

Lots of love,
Nan xx

....

From: nancyblue#@aol.com
To: georgie*harris@hotmail.com
Date: Thur, 17 August 02:15
Subject: The Searchers . . .

Did you know there's a type of racing car engine called a Jeff Harris? And a shop in Wyoming called Jeff Harris Feeds? My eyes must have turned quite square from all this staring at the screen so I'm off to bed. Will resume my search tomorrow, or rather later today, as it's now 2.15 in the morning . . .

Nx

....

From: georgie*harris@hotmail.com
To: nancyblue#@aol.com
Date: Thur, 17 August 17:25
Subject: Re: The Searchers . . .

Dear Nan,

Thank you so much for helping me search – it's a nightmare isn't it!! I must have gone through thousands this afternoon, even the ones I know aren't to do with my dad – like the Jeff Harris Donkey Sanctuary on the Isle of Man – just in case. You're right, I should try and talk to someone who knew him but I just don't know who. My dad was an only child and I haven't seen his parents since my mum married Tone-Deaf. All I can remember is that they lived near a river somewhere in Surrey and their house had stairs going up the outside of the building! And my grandma had a really cool dolls' house with a toy monkey on the roof. Angelica will probably know the address but I don't think I can ask her at the moment. Things are still really crappy at home.

Last night I was going through my lines at the kitchen table when Tone-Deaf came in for his tea. 'Ooh, it's the actress,' he said, dead sarcastic and then he kept getting Michaela to say 'Romeo, Romeo!' to me in a really stupid voice. For a moment I really hated her because she didn't feel like my sister at all, but the evil baddy's horrible mini sidekick. Then my mum told her to be quiet and there was this awful silence. Tone-Deaf picked up his plate and tipped his tea into the sink. 'Don't speak to my daughter like that ever again,' he said to Angelica, his voice all menacing and low. And then he said to Michaela, 'Come on, Princess, we're going to McDonald's.' It was horrible, as if our so-called family had been split right down the middle. But when I got up to give my mum a hug she just walked out of the room and said, 'Leave it, Georgie.'

So you see she's obviously still mad at me for going behind her back and getting those leaflets. There's no way she'd let me talk to my grandparents. I guess the internet is my only hope.

But before I go I must quickly tell you the terrible thing that happened today. It was the dress rehearsal for the show and I really messed up. I came in too early for my song and I kept forgetting my lines. Jamie was dead nice about it and gave me another one of his hugs but I could see Debbie was looking really stressed. Do you have any expert advice on staying calm? If I messed up like that in the dress rehearsal how am I going to get through the performance in front of a massive audience? And more importantly, in front of my own mum?! I haven't plucked up the courage to ask her if she'll come yet.

I was going to ask her tonight. What do you think I should do? After today's performance I'm not so sure. Tone-Deaf has put her through hell to let me come to the workshop, if I blow it in front of her tomorrow night it will have all been for nothing! Please, please email me your advice . . .

Lots of love,
Georgie xxx

....

From: nancyblue#@aol.com
To: georgie*harris@hotmail.com
Date: Thur, 17 August 17:27
Subject: Re: The Searchers . . .

Darling I'm here – I'm online too, still searching furiously for your dad! Have you come across the male model called Jeff Harris who belongs to the Unicorn Modelling Agency by the way? What a stud muffin!!

Will compose some top tips on staying calm right now – just wanted you to know I'm online.

Nx

From: georgie*harris@hotmail.com
To: nancyblue#@aol.com
Date: Thur, 17 August 17:28
Subject: Re: The Searchers . . .

Hurrah!! Can't believe you're searching too. That is so frost-free!

Thank you!

Gx

....

From: nancyblue#@aol.com
To: georgie*harris@hotmail.com
Date: Thur, 17 August 17:30
Subject: Re: The Searchers . . .

First things first – having a lousy dress rehearsal is a very good sign, believe it or not. Superstition has it (and believe me superstition is the lifeblood of the theatre world) that if your dress rehearsal goes well the actual show will bomb. By messing up you did Debbie and your cast members a huge favour, so give yourself a big congratulatory hug, darling. Go on – right now – who cares if you're in the library!

Nx

....

From: georgie*harris@hotmail.com
To: nancyblue#@aol.com
Date: Thur, 17 August 17:31
Subject: Re: The Searchers . . .

OK – I've done it, I've given myself a hug and now the man opposite is staring over his glasses at me like I'm a freak! Are you sure messing up is a good omen? It doesn't make any sense!

Gx

....

From: nancyblue#@aol.com
To: georgie*harris@hotmail.com
Date: Thur, 17 August 17:39
Subject: Re: The Searchers . . .

Oh Georgie, darling, nothing makes any sense when it comes to the world of acting. Look at what we do for a start – dressing up in costumes and pretending to be other people. Driving ourselves nuts trying to 'get into character' and 'find our motivation' and all that jazz. It's a crazy world where ordinary rules do not apply so yes, you messing up is a very good omen indeed. I think you most definitely should ask your mum to come. I'm sure once she sees you perform she will be awash with pride and all the rubbish she's had to endure this week from TD will all seem worthwhile. I'll never forget the first time I watched Dylan in a school play. He was only about five and only had to say one line but I can still remember it to this day: 'Thank you for coming to our play.' Only he got overwhelmed by the enormity of the occasion and said, 'Thank you for coming out to play.' It was so cute and brought the house down. And I didn't mind in the least that he messed it up, I was just so damned proud that he was my son. Your mum will feel exactly the same, you'll see.

OK, tips for staying calm:

When you are waiting back stage to make your first entrance
take some time to get in the zone. *Become* Blousey and block
everything and everyone else out.
Take deep breaths to try and slow your heart rate, but not
so deep that you pass out!
When you get out on stage have fun — it's such a fun show
after all, so enjoy!
Feed off the audience as if their laughter and applause are
oxygen — let their energy lift you and your performance.
Be proud — you would never have been cast as Blousey if
your teacher didn't think you were up to it — so rise to the
occasion.

I hope that helps, darling, and do break a leg! There's
another ridiculous theatrical tradition for you, apparently
it's very bad luck to wish an actor good luck!! Will be
thinking of you.

Nx

....

From: georgie*harris@hotmail.com
To: nancyblue#@aol.com
Date: Thur, 17 August 17:42
Subject: Re: The Searchers . . .

Thank you!!! God I am so nervous I think I might be sick. Going to do five more minutes searching and then get back home to rehearse. I can't forget my lines tomorrow. I can't. Part of me wishes I COULD break my leg – then at least I'd get out of the show. Thank you so much for your help.

Lots of love,
Georgie xx

....

From: nancyblue#@aol.com
To: georgie*harris@hotmail.com
Date: Thur, 17 August 17:43
Subject: Re: The Searchers . . .

You're welcome, darling, and you'll be fine. Will be thinking of you . . .

All my love,

Nx

....

From: georgie*harris@hotmail.com
To: nancyblue#@aol.com
Date: Fri, 18 August 09:09
Subject: Good Morning!

Just thought I'd email you on my way to the workshop. We don't have to be in till 10 this morning because Debbie thought we might need a lie-in after all of our hard work. It feels like I have ten thousand Tiggers all bouncing around at a disco inside of me, I'm so scared and excited. Guess what? My mum said she'd come to the show tonight!

Tone-Deaf was out at work all last night and I was sitting on my bed going through my lines for about the millionth time when Angelica popped her head around the door. 'Do you need any help with that?' she asked, nodding towards my script. I couldn't believe it! When I'd stopped my mouth from gaping in shock I smiled and said yes and she came and sat on the end of my bed. 'Do you want me to test you on your lines?' she asked, but the way she said it was all sort of shy and sweet, as if she was really asking me if I still wanted to be her friend. 'Yes please,' I replied. And then she looked at me and her lovely big eyes were all glassy with tears and I didn't know what to do because last time I tried to hug her she told me to leave it. So I just put my hand over hers on the bed, the way Jamie did with mine that night in the woods. Angelica didn't say anything but then she turned her hand over and laced her fingers through mine and she gripped it so tightly I knew exactly what she wanted to say. So I gripped back just as tightly in return and then I said, dead quietly, 'Would you like to come to see the show tomorrow night?' And she nodded and said, 'Yes, I'd like that very much,' and a tear spilled over the rim of her eye and made a shimmering trail all down her cheek.

Later, when I was lying in bed hugging Hendrix, I felt so happy. I know things aren't really fixed. And I know I still haven't found out the truth about my dad. But my mum is coming to the show. My mum still loves me and I've got you and Jamie too. Oprah was talking about gratitude the other day, saying that we should make more time to appreciate the little things in our lives, like the smell of coffee. Personally I hate the smell of coffee so I can't say I'm really grateful for that, but today, walking through the park and watching the birds swooping like miniature feathered kites in and out of the trees, I felt so grateful. For this one day at least I can pretend that I am normal. I can pretend that I am the kind of girl who gets a lead role in a play and has a boy interested in her and a parent who really cares.

Hope you have a lovely day too and I'll email you tomorrow to let you know how the show goes tonight.

Lots of love,
Georgie xx

....

From: nancyblue#@aol.com
To: georgie*harris@hotmail.com
Date: Fri, 18 August 10:26
Subject: Re: Good Morning!

Well, good morning indeed! What excellent news. I can't tell you how pleased I am that your mum is coming to the show. I only wish I could be there too. But I will be there in spirit, believe me! And what on earth do you mean, you can 'pretend' you are the kind of girl who gets a lead role and a boy interested in her? You're not pretending at all, darling — it's all real. And you thoroughly deserve it. And of course your mum really cares. It's like I told you when we met up – she is trapped in an abusive relationship with a bullying partner. Her behaviour is not that of someone who doesn't care, it's of someone who is scared and desperately trying to hold it all together. All your talk of dress rehearsals and performances is really quite infectious, sweetie. I think I'm going to ring Bing today and tell him to put me up for a small part somewhere, nothing major, just a couple of lines or something. See how I do. You've given me the acting bug I'm afraid. Have a great evening – break both legs!!!

Lots of love,
Nan x

....

From: georgie*harris@hotmail.com
To: nancyblue#@aol.com
Date: Fri, 18 August 18:13
Subject: Good morning – Bad evening . . .

Oh Nan – I just tried calling you but you weren't home. I really need to speak to you. I'm going to send you this email so I can get everything off my chest and then I'll try and imagine what you would tell me to do.

It's 6 o'clock. The show starts in one hour and everything has gone wrong. Again. When I got back from rehearsals today Tone-Deaf's cab was on the driveway and he was fiddling about with the engine. I should have known something was up when he actually said hello to me – and in his dead friendly 'Michaela voice' too. I said hello and went straight into the kitchen. Michaela was dancing around all excited with one of her cuddly Tiggers. Angelica was sat at the table looking down at her hands. 'We're going to a show, Georgie, we're going to a show!' Michaela cried. I thought she was talking about Bugsy Malone. 'I know,' I said, picking her up and swirling her around, 'and Debbie is saving you a seat right at the front so you can see everything properly.' Michaela looked at me with wide eyes, 'Is Debbie coming to Winnie-the-Pooh too?' I still didn't realise what had happened. 'No, silly, the show isn't Winnie-the-Pooh, it's Bugsy Malone.' Michaela wriggled down from my arms and ran over to Angelica, 'It's not Bugsy Malone, is it Mum? It's Winnie-the-Pooh.' I looked at Angelica but she just kept staring down at her hands and then she slowly nodded. 'What do you mean?' I asked, sitting down at the table opposite her. 'What's she talking about?'

'Daddy's taking us to see the Winnie-the-Pooh show up in London,' Michaela said. 'You're coming too, Georgie, we're all going.' I looked at Angelica in shock. 'What do you mean? Tonight?' Again she nodded. 'But we can't! What about Bugsy Malone?' Finally Angelica looked at me. 'I'm sorry,' she muttered, 'he's got the tickets, I'm going to have to go.' I felt like I was going to be sick all over the table. 'What about me,' I gasped, like a stupid little kid. Angelica gave me a feeble smile. 'It's OK, I've told him you're doing your own show and can't come,' she replied, as if this somehow made it all right. 'But you won't be coming?' I asked, a huge ball of uncried sobs welling at the back of my throat. She shook her head and looked back down again. I wanted to yell at her. I wanted to say, 'but I've got one of the main parts. I'm your daughter too, why does it always have to be about Michaela and him?' I wanted to say, 'I hate you, you pathetic wimp.' But it was as if the sobs at the back of my throat had formed a seal and nothing could get out. I stood up. I went upstairs. I brushed my teeth and washed my face and got changed. Then I walked back down the stairs and, without calling out goodbye or anything, I opened the front door and let myself out. 'Off out are we?' Tone-Deaf called after me, his voice all mockingly cheerful, as if what he was really saying was, 'Ha, ha, I won!' I ignored him and kept on walking. I kept on walking till I got to the high street, where I tried to phone you. And now I'm in the internet café typing this and I don't know what to do.

I was so excited she was coming, Nan, but she's let me down yet again. Why did she bother saying she'd come if she didn't really mean it? Why does she always let him get his own way in the end? He must really hate me, mustn't he, to have done this? We never go out to shows together as a family. Ever. He knew it was my big night tonight and so he had to go and ruin it.

I'm trying to guess what you would tell me to do but my mind is completely blank. I suppose Oprah would say I should be grateful for what I have got. Well, I'm breathing in the smell of the coffee from the internet café and trying my hardest to feel grateful, but it's just making me feel sick. Perhaps you would tell me that the show must go on? That I should hold my head up high and give my best ever performance. I think you would tell me that I am fabulous. I think you would tell me that if I let this ruin my performance I will be letting Tone-Deaf win. Well, you would be right. He might be able to crush my mum, but he will never beat me.

I AM FABULOUS
I AM FABULOUS
I AM FABULOUS

I'm going to head off to the community centre now and sit under the willow tree for a bit. My mind is racing so fast I need to go somewhere quiet and calm. But whatever happens I won't let him beat me, Nan, don't worry.

Lots of love,
Georgie xx

Part Five

The Show Goes On

Drat and double drat! Why am I never around when you need me most? I'm so sorry I wasn't here to take your call earlier, I'd gone salsa dancing with Ricardo. Georgie, darling, for once I am totally and utterly speechless. Of all the mean-spirited, nasty things that man could have done. I am so pleased you didn't let him get the better of you though. I hope you gave the performance of your life and everyone loved you. You were spot on about what I would have said to you. But I would have added one more thing – I am sure you still had one parent watching you perform. I hope that you sensed the spirit of your dad with you tonight, watching and cheering you on from the wings.

Once again, Georgie, if you need me for anything please call or email me. And please let me know how you got on.

Am thinking of you and sending you an email attachment of courage and love.

All my love,
Nan xxx

From: nancyblue#@aol.com
To: georgie*harris@hotmail.com
Date: Sat, 19 August 11:15
Subject: R U OK?

Is everything OK? Please email me or call me as soon as you can to let me know how the show went.

Lots of love from your most impatient friend,
Nan xx

From: nancyblue#@aol.com
To: georgie*harris@hotmail.com
Date: Sat, 19 August 22:04
Subject: Hello . . .

Oh dear. It's now gone 10 o'clock at night and still no word from you. I do wish you had a mobile so that I could call you. I guess I'll have to wait until tomorrow. I really hope everything is OK . . .

Nan xxx

....

From: georgie*harris@hotmail.com
To: nancyblue#@aol.com
Date: Sun, 20 August 14:12
Subject: Amazing news!!!

You are not going to believe what has happened!!! And how much has happened!!! I can hardly fit it all in my head there's so much, so who knows how I'm going to fit it into an email! It's weird because the first thing that happened on Friday night was amazing enough on its own. But then something else happened that was even more amazing. At first it seemed like it was going to be really bad but then it changed and – oh God, I just don't know how I'm going to tell you all of this.

OK, I've taken a deep breath and I've warmed up my typing fingers and I'm going to tell you it all right from the start, but I can tell you now, never in your wildest dreams will you be able to guess what I am about to write.

After I emailed you on Friday night I went to the duck pond and sat there for a while, waiting for the others to start arriving and trying to get my head together. I was so upset about what had happened at home and so disappointed that Angelica wouldn't be there to see me perform. I kept thinking of you, but every time I tried to tell myself that I was fabulous I only got as far as the 'fab' bit before letting out a sob. And 'I AM FAB-BOO HOO' doesn't make you feel that great at all! Then I saw this little duck drifting across the pond all by itself and it made me feel even worse because it reminded me of me – all alone – and I started to cry even more. Until I heard a crunch on the dry grass behind me and Jamie say, 'Blousey, what's up?' It was too late for me to pretend I wasn't crying so I just sat there sniffing and sobbing like a baby until I felt his arm around my shoulders and him pulling me in to his chest. Oh Nan, it was so horrible and lovely all at the same time, a bit like those American chocolates with the peanut butter filling. And although part of me wanted to pull out of his arms and run away in embarrassment, most of me wanted to stay exactly where I was. Because it was so nice to be held, and have my hair stroked, and hear Jamie's soft gruff voice. 'It's all right,' he kept whispering over and over again. 'I'm here.' And then, when he asked me what was wrong, I couldn't hold it in any longer. I felt so tired of having to pretend all the time. Having to pretend that everything's OK and that I'm cool and sophisticated and have a totally normal family, when actually everything, including me, is broken.

So I told him. About my mum and Tone-Deaf and about how I'm sick of trying to do the right thing and not upset anyone and feeling like the outsider in my own family. And then I told him how Tone-Deaf had smashed up the bathroom and pulled my hair and bruised my arm and how, just when things were starting to look up, he ruined everything by not letting my mum or Michaela come to the show. Jamie kept on holding me the whole time, not saying a word, and then, when I'd finally finished, he sat back a little so that he could look straight into my eyes. And then he kissed me.

Yes, you did read that last bit correctly – JAMIE PHELPS KISSED ME – and yes, it was a proper kiss, on the lips. It was really lovely and soft too, as if one of the butterflies had fluttered free from my tummy and settled on my mouth. And the funniest thing of all was I hadn't even done any of that stuff you recommended. I hadn't licked my lips or done that triangle gaze or giggled or looked at him through lowered lashes – my eyes were way too full of tears for that! But he still kissed me! And then he wiped the tears from my cheeks and he said, 'Don't worry, Blousey, I'll take care of you.' And then he told me that after the show I wouldn't have to go back home because I could come to his and that once he'd told his parents what had happened he was sure they'd be fine about me staying for as long as I liked. I knew that it wasn't really the answer to my problems. I knew that I couldn't just move into Jamie's house and live happily ever after, but I was so happy and excited that he'd kissed me I didn't care. I wonder if how I felt is what it's like to be drunk, because when we stood up to go into the community centre I felt all wobbly and my head was spinning. Thankfully I managed to 'sober up' before the performance though! And in the end it didn't really matter that my mum wasn't there because it was so nice acting next to Jamie and seeing his proud smile after I sang my solo and feeling him squeeze my hand when we took our bows. When the audience started to applaud it was like being hit by a wall of noise and I remembered what you'd once said to me about my life not always being run by adults and how one day I would be free. At that moment, staring out at the rows of smiling, cheering faces, I got a taste of that freedom because they were all clapping and cheering me for something I'd done all by myself and in the end not even Tone-Deaf had managed to stop me.

But as soon as the show was over and the audience had all filed out I started feeling sick again. How could I go back to Jamie's house? I'd only been there once before, what would his parents think? But how could I go home? Jamie seemed really happy though and he kept hugging me and telling me how well I'd done, so I didn't know what to do. But, just as we were coming out of the community centre and heading to the car park to find his parents, I felt someone tap me on the shoulder. You'll never guess who it was, Nan – Angelica! I almost didn't recognise her because she was wearing a huge pair of sunglasses. As soon as I said 'Mum!' Jamie stopped and turned and I felt a stab of fear. I was really worried he'd say something about what I'd told him. Can you imagine if he'd have had a go at her? It would have been horrible. But it was fine, he just nodded and smiled. Then Angelica smiled back and said, 'You were both great, really great.' Yes, you read that right, Nan, SHE'D ACTUALLY BEEN TO THE SHOW!!!

I looked at her face in shock but couldn't make out what was going on behind the sunglasses. So I asked her if she'd seen the show and she nodded. Just then a car pulled up. It was Jamie's mum. She smiled and said well done, then she asked Jamie if he wanted a lift home. He looked at me and then at my mum. 'I don't know,' he replied. 'What are you doing, Blousey?' I felt sick. I so badly wanted to go with him but then I couldn't very well leave my mum on her own after she'd come to the show. I had to find out what had happened. I was also a bit worried about why she was wearing huge sunglasses at night. 'I'd better go with my mum,' I muttered, hoping he would understand. Jamie nodded. 'If you need me give me a ring, yeah?' he replied before staring hard at Angelica. She looked down at the floor. Jamie kissed me on the cheek, then slipped into the back of his mum's car and they drove off.

So then I turned to Angelica. 'How did you manage to come?' was all I could say. She looked at me and pointed to the shadowy hollow beneath the willow tree. 'Can we go and talk?' I nodded and followed her across the bank of the pond. It was so weird, Nan, going with her to the very same spot where Jamie had kissed me. It was a lot colder by then though, and the reflection of the moon was floating on the surface like a giant glitter ball. We both sat down on the stubbly ground and Angelica turned to face me. 'You were wonderful, Georgie,' she said quietly. 'Your voice, it's so powerful. It was like watching –' She fell silent and gazed into space. 'It was like watching what?' I asked. 'Your dad,' she replied. 'He had an amazing voice too.' I followed her gaze across the pond and then, for some strange reason, I started humming Wonderful Tonight. 'Stop it!' she said, turning back to face me, and then she started to cry. 'What's wrong?' I asked, but she just kept crying. It was horrible, Nan, I've never seen her cry like that before. I was starting to get really scared. 'It was like part of him had come back to life, seeing you on that stage,' she said, 'and I'd forgotten . . .'

I hardly dared breathe. What had she forgotten? 'How talented he was,' she continued. 'And how lovely.' Then she gave this tiny smile. But I was really confused. If my dad was so lovely then how come she let Tone-Deaf say all that stuff about him being on drugs? It took all of my courage to ask her, Nan, I was so relieved to hear her say something nice about my dad I didn't want to ruin it, but I had to find out the truth. I can't remember exactly how I asked her – I was so nervous my words tumbled out of my mouth in the completely wrong order. But she obviously understood what I was getting at. 'Tony's very good at twisting things,' she said. 'He gets me so that I don't know what to believe.' I couldn't help frowning. 'But you knew Dad – you knew he wasn't on drugs. Didn't you? Mum?' She started crying again, but this time the sobs were a lot gentler, as if the sadness inside her had worn itself out. I moved a little bit down the bank so that I was crouched right in front of her and I took hold of her hands. 'Mum! Dad wasn't on drugs was he? Tony was lying. He was just trying to make me feel bad, he —'

'He wasn't lying, Georgie,' she interrupted, pulling her hands from mine. I rocked back on my heels in shock. 'What? But —'

'Your dad did take drugs, the same as lots of people took drugs in the job he was in. But it was only dope, it wasn't anything heavy.' I stared at her, at the shields of black covering her eyes. 'But that day, the day he died, did he? Had he taken drugs then?' Angelica nodded. 'Yes. But it wasn't like Tony said. It wasn't because he didn't care about us. He'd smoked a joint, but he wasn't out of it. That wasn't what killed him, Georgie, it was the rain on the road. It made the bike skid.'

I swallowed hard. 'So why did you let Tony say that stuff about him not loving us and not caring if he died.' Angelica turned away, and when she spoke her voice was barely more than a whisper. 'Because he'd made me believe it was true.' She turned back to face me. 'I know it sounds horrible but I was so angry when your dad died. I felt like he'd abandoned us and I felt so helpless without him. I was a complete mess, but then Tony came along and he seemed so caring and strong –' I couldn't help giving a sarcastic snort of laughter at this. Caring and strong?!! What was wrong with her? She was making him sound like some kind of superhero – like Batman, or Pa from Little House on the Prairie. 'All he cares about is himself and his stupid football team!' I shouted – and this time my words all came out in exactly the right order. Angelica looked away. 'He DID seem caring at first. I wouldn't have got together with him if he didn't. Then he started saying stuff, about your dad, about how he couldn't believe he had smoked drugs before he rode his bike and how he obviously didn't care about me and you. I let him twist everything.' I shook my head in disbelief, 'But why? How could you?' Angelica sighed. 'Because it was easier if I made myself hate your dad. It didn't hurt so much. But when I saw you tonight –' she broke off again. 'When you saw me what?' I asked. 'Well it made me remember that Jeff wasn't a bad person at all. He was funny and talented and such a force of nature. Just like you, Georgie.'

It was really weird, Nan. Like being told that what I thought was my life was actually just a dream. My dad WAS a nice person and my mum DID love him. And she loved me, or at least it seemed as if she did. I grabbed hold of her hands. 'Leave him, Mum. Leave Tony. We'll be OK, the three of us. I'll help you. I'll get a part-time job, I'll –' But once again she pulled her hands from mine and turned away. 'How can I leave him?' she cried. 'You don't understand. He'd kill me if I took Michaela away from him and I can't leave her. I can't leave my little girl.' I stared hard at her. I think that's when I knew something really bad had happened. 'Why are you wearing those sunglasses? What happened tonight? What did he say when you told him you were coming here? What did he do?' She bowed her head and didn't say a word. 'Mum? Take off the sunglasses. I want to see your face.' She shook her head. 'No – I've been crying, my eyes are –'

Before she had the chance to stop me I reached across and pulled the glasses from her head. Both of her eyes, her beautiful huge grey eyes, had shrunk to the size of currants, ringed by swollen bruises. It was so shocking, Nan, you wouldn't believe how horrible they looked. 'Oh my God, Mum! What has he done to you?' She looked at me through the puffy skin. 'Now do you see? How can I leave him when he's capable of something like this?' What she said seemed all topsy turvy. How could she *stay* with him when he was capable of something like this? I moved so that I was right next to her and put my arm around her tiny shoulders. 'We could run away,' I suggested. 'We could go to one of those refuge places like in the leaflets I gave you.' Angelica shook her head and grabbed the sunglasses back from me. 'I still can't believe you went and told a complete stranger our business,' she said. I frowned. How could she start telling me off when all I was trying to do was help her? 'It wasn't a stranger, Mum, it was a friend.' Angelica put the sunglasses back on and I didn't try to stop her. 'I thought you said it was your friend's mum,' she replied. I took a deep breath and decided to tell her the truth. It was really hard, Nan, but I didn't know what else I could do. 'Yeah, well I only said that to make you feel better. It was actually a friend of mine, but she's a mum too and she's really wise and she's just lost her husband so she knows what it's like to lose someone you love. You'd really like her, Mum. She's called Nan and she used to be an actress and she's already said that she'd like to help us in any way she can so maybe –'

Angelica turned to face me, brushing my arm from her shoulders. 'How do you know this person, Georgie?' Her voice was newsreader-serious. I forced myself to smile to make her see that it was no big deal. 'We met on the internet. It's a long story but –'

'On the internet? Oh my God, what have I told you about visiting those chatrooms? You could be talking to anyone.'

I frowned and shook my head. 'No, it's OK because I've met her in real life too, so I know she's for real. Although she did pretend to be someone else when we first met, but that was OK because it was just her son and she was supposed to be pretending to be him because she was answering his emails.' I could feel Angelica getting tenser and tenser beside me so I carried on, trying to put her mind at ease. 'At first I was a bit cross with her for tricking me but she was so nice and gave me so much advice about my acting and boys and stuff that I was actually pleased I'd been emailing her and not Dylan.' I stopped and waited to see what Angelica would say. 'Dylan?' she replied in a tight little voice. 'Yes,' I said. 'Her son's Dylan Curtland – he used to play Jimmy in Jessop Close. You know? The one who worked in the abattoir and got electrocuted on a toaster.' I sat back and waited, sure that this piece of news would console her for once and for all. But it only made her worse.

'I don't believe it!' she cried, standing up. 'How could you confide in a complete stranger? How could you tell someone you don't even know about our personal business?' A spark of anger lit up inside me. 'Well who else was I supposed to tell?' I replied, standing up too and, because she was standing further down the bank from me, I was the tallest. 'I didn't have anyone, Mum. I was lonely.' Angelica looked at me as if I was insane. 'Didn't have anyone? What about me? I'm your mother. Why couldn't you have come and talked to me?' I started to laugh at this point but I didn't really find what she said funny at all. 'How could I talk to you? You're –' I stopped myself just in time. 'What?' she asked, and I could see her mouth was trembling. I looked at the ground. 'I thought you had enough to deal with. I was scared if I came to you with my problems it would make you get . . . sick.' 'Sick? What do you mean, sick?' she said. I didn't want to say it, Nan, but I knew it was now or never. 'You know. Drunk, sick.'

I glanced at her, stood in front of me, shorter than me, thinner than me, clasping her hands in front of her, just like a child, and I wanted to scream, you're the mum, you know, YOU'RE the one who should be looking after ME. But I swallowed the thought back down and waited for her to say something. She looked this way and that around the deserted community centre and then she looked straight at me. 'Come on,' she said, her voice quiet but deadly firm. I gulped. 'Where to?' For a horrible moment I thought she was going to take me back home, back to that psycho, even after everything he'd done to her. And then I thought about what he might do to me for being in the show and causing so much trouble and I felt sicker than I've ever felt in my life before. 'Just come,' she said, taking hold of my hand. And although it was still really warm outside, her fingers were as cold as ice. 'I can't go back home, Mum. I can't go back to him,' I began pleading, my voice rising in panic. 'We're not,' she said as she gently pulled on my hand. Shivering with fear I followed her out on to the high street and past the grey stone church. Where was she taking me if we weren't going home? The clock on the church tower started to strike 11 and somewhere in the distance someone started to laugh loudly, like a demented clown. 'Where are we going?' I asked again, tears burning at the sides of my eyes. I decided to make a run for it if she started heading home. I didn't care if I had to go all the way to Jamie's house, or sleep rough in the park, or even run all the way to you in Hove, I was not going back there. But as we got level with the ice-cream parlour Angelica turned down a side road. I frowned, there was nothing down there apart from houses and – I spotted the old-fashioned blue street lamp and froze. Guess where she was taking me, Nan? The police station.

At first I was terrified. I thought she was going to report you for emailing me. 'I can't,' I said, rooted to the spot. Angelica let out a huge sigh and said, 'I thought you wanted me to do something?' I stared at her, confused. 'Do something about what?' 'About Tony,' she replied. It took a few moments for what she was saying to filter through to the part of my brain that makes sense of stuff. 'Are you serious?' I whispered. Angelica took off her sunglasses and despite the puffiness and the bruising I don't think she'd ever looked more beautiful or brave. She nodded and I saw a tear trickle down her swollen cheek, shimmering in the blue of the police light. 'I'm so sorry,' she whispered and then, I don't quite know how, we were hugging and she was rocking me gently from side to side. And I felt like I finally had my mum back, and it was so lovely and I felt so safe, I never wanted to let her go. When we finally pulled apart and looked at each other we had both been crying, but we were smiling too, real smiles that reached our watery eyes.

So there you go. I knew it would take ages to tell you it all, but I just had to let you know. Can you believe that so much could happen in just one night?! Jamie kissed me, we did the show, my mum came to the show and then she left Tone-Deaf!

When we went into the police station they interviewed Angelica and then they sent a car round to arrest Tone-Deaf. I'm not sure what's happened to him, but the police brought Michaela to us and then they took us all to this refuge in a place called West Drayton. All three of us are sharing a room which is actually kind of cool, like we're on holiday in a caravan or something. There are other women here with their kids too – all of us hiding from psycho men – which is actually kind of depressing. But the best thing about it is the computer room, where I am right now. It's funny, when I think of how hard I've longed to have a computer I could use in my own house, I never meant for it to be like this! I'll be in touch again soon, when I know more about what's happening.

Lots of love,
Georgie xx

....

From: nancyblue#@aol.com
To: georgie*harris@hotmail.com
Date: Sun, 20 August 09:01
Subject: Re: Amazing news!!!

Oh my goodness! Yet again you have rendered me speechless. Well, maybe not quite. First things first – would it be possible for me to talk to your mum? Just to put her mind at rest and reassure her that I'm not some kind of internet stalker of teenagers! The last thing I want to do is add to her worries. Maybe I could come up and visit you? Or you could all come down here? If you and your mum and sister need somewhere to stay, Georgie, I'd be only too happy to help out. There's plenty of room here with just Woodstock and me rattling about. Please give your mum my number and try and get her to call me.

Well, you must be feeling pretty strange right now, darling, what with everything that's happened. What have the police done with Tone-Deaf? I hope they lock him up and throw away the key. And what about Jamie? Your description of his kiss brought a tear to my eye, well, quite a few tears if truth be told! Are you able to contact him where you are? I do so hope so. He sounds lovely, kind and strong – just the kind of person you need right now.

Do you have a phone number at the refuge? I could call you if you like? I feel so useless all the way down here. Just let me know what you would like me to do. And don't forget to have a word with your mum . . .

Speak soon I hope.

All my love,
Nan xxx

....

From: georgie*harris@hotmail.com
To: nancyblue#@aol.com
Date: Mon, 21 August 11:14
Subject: Terrible news

Hi Nan,

You are never going to believe what has happened. My stomach is in knots and my face is burning – but out of rage not embarrassment. Tone-Deaf has been released on bail! The police have charged him with actual bodily harm, but he's been freed until the court case. Angelica went hysterical when she found out. She says we'll never be able to go back home now and Michaela keeps crying because she wants her Tiggers. In the rush to get away we weren't able to get any of our things. My mum is too scared to go back to work in case Tone-Deaf turns up there, so we're not going to have any money either. The police told us that Tone-Deaf's bail conditions mean he can't come anywhere near the house or any of us and he has to stay at his mum's down in Mile End, but there's no way he'll do that. He's going to be going mental about Angelica reporting him to the police, I know he is. I wanted to call you today to have a chat about it but I didn't dare ask Angelica. She was so annoyed with me for emailing you there's no way she'd let me use her mobile to call you. I don't think she'd like it if you rang her either — she's too stressed out to think straight. She did let me call Jamie though, so I managed to explain to him what had happened and how we'd had to go into hiding.

It sounds so exciting doesn't it, going into hiding. But actually it isn't exciting at all. It's scary and boring and this place stinks of disinfectant and boiled vegetables. It's like being in a hospital or prison and at night-time you hear all these weird noises — doors slamming and people you don't know walking down the corridor and babies you don't know crying and I hate it. It isn't fair. Why should we be the ones who end up in prison while Tone-Deaf is walking around free? Angelica even started saying she was going to drop the charges. I went mad when she did though. Why should he get away with what he did? Why should he be allowed to hurt women and children? I wish my dad was still alive, then none of this would have happened. I am so scared. I didn't tell Angelica because I'm trying to keep her strong, but a voice in my head keeps asking, what if he gets let off? What will happen to us then? How will we ever be free of him?

Jamie was dead concerned on the phone and he said that if I ever needed anywhere to stay I could always go to his. It's so nice thinking I have you both caring for me.

I don't really know what's going to happen, Nan, but I promise I'll keep you posted and if I get a chance to call you I promise I will.

Lots of love,
Your imprisoned e-mate,
Georgie xxx

....

From: nancyblue#@aol.com
To: georgie*harris@hotmail.com
Date: Mon, 21 August 13:24
Subject: Re: Terrible news

This is scandalous. How can that monster be free to walk the streets while you all have to hide away like criminals? Try to stay strong, Georgie, and know that you always have somewhere to come if you need to. I understand that you don't want to upset your mum at this time, but please remember my invitation, and if you feel it would help, then please do get her to call me. Remember what I told you about life being like a book and how the bad chapters never last forever. They always come to a close eventually and often there is something truly wonderful waiting for you on the very next page. Please let me know if there is anything I can do for you – all of you.

All my love and a great big cyber hug!
Nan xxx

....

From: georgie*harris@hotmail.com
To: nancyblue#@aol.com
Date: Tue, 22 August 09:04
Subject: Going Home

Hi Nan,

Just thought I'd send you a quick email to let you know the latest. We're going home. Last night a really nice police lady came to talk to Angelica and she told us it was completely safe for us to go back to Ruislip and that if Tone-Deaf turned up we could page the police on this special pager thing and they would be straight round. Angelica gave her a smile as she took the pager, but I could see from her eyes that she was still dead scared, even through all the bruising. And I'm scared too. But I guess we don't have a choice. All of our stuff is there. This is really gross, but I've been wearing the same clothes since Friday! I'm desperate to see Jamie too. I hope it will be OK, I hope Tone-Deaf stays away, but I have this really heavy feeling in the pit of my stomach. Even though the police said Tone-Deaf would go to jail if he came anywhere near us, I still can't relax. When he gets mad it's like he loses all control. Like that day in the bathroom when he smashed the shower door. I'm so scared he'll lose control again and come to the house. And then what will happen?

Better go, can hear Angelica calling. Will email you soon, I promise.

Lots of love,
G xxx

....

From: nancyblue#@aol.com
To: georgie*harris@hotmail.com
Date: Tue, 22 August 10:18
Subject: Re: Going Home

Don't worry, Georgie, I'm sure it will be fine. Tone-Deaf isn't going to risk going to jail for breaking his bail conditions. Remember, he is a typical bully and all bullies are cowards at heart. I'm sure the prospect of jail absolutely terrifies him. I am thinking of you, darling, all the time, and praying that you and your sister and mum stay safe. I have an audition this afternoon. Nothing exciting, just a bit part playing a witch in a children's TV show! Not quite the glamour role I was hoping for but still, at least I'll be dipping my toe back in the acting pond.

Please let me know when you're home safe, darling.

All my love,
Nan xx

....

From: georgie*harris@hotmail.com
To: nancyblue#@aol.com
Date: Wed, 23 August 11:08
Subject: Oh my God!!

Oh my God – you had an audition!! How did you get on? Did you get the part? Which kids' show is it? I'm a bit of an expert on kids' shows thanks to Michaela! It would be so cool if it was a programme she watched, then I could show off to her and say, 'I know that witch!'

Going home was so weird. Even though we'd only been away a few days the house seemed really different when we walked through the door. Empty and dead – if it's possible for houses to die? I think Angelica noticed it too because I saw her shiver as she looked around the hall. As soon as we got settled she called a locksmith and arranged for someone to come round and change all the locks. Last night we all slept together again, Michaela and I topped and tailed in her bed and Angelica had mine. I slept even worse than I did in the refuge, waking up every hour to check the other two were OK. And then, when I did fall asleep, I had horrible dreams about Jessica and Kate One forming a rock band with Tone-Deaf!

Please let me know how you got on in your audition. I'm feeling a lot better today, now that the locks are changed. And Jamie's coming round later. I don't like leaving the other two on their own right now, just in case. Oh well, better go and get the food shopping for Angelica and get back.

Lots of love,
Georgie xx

....

From: nancyblue#@aol.com
To: georgie*harris@hotmail.com
Date: Wed, 23 August 15:59
Subject: Re: Oh my God!!

So pleased you're all home safe, darling. I'm sure you really have no need to worry, so stay strong. And enjoy your visit with Jamie lolwaw (laughing out loud with a wink!). I got the part I auditioned for – though I have slightly mixed feelings about it. I'm playing a witch called Wisteria in a show called Tales From the Cauldron. Oh how I wish I could put a spell on Tone-Deaf – turn him into a slug or something, and then tread on him! Perhaps I should invest in a book on witchcraft and try it out – all part of getting into character you understand! Well, do keep me up to date with events and don't forget, just let me know if you need anything or if you think I should talk to your mum.

All my love,
The wicked witch of the south!
xx

....

From: georgie*harris@hotmail.com
To: nancyblue#@aol.com
Date: Thur, 24 August 10:47
Subject: Horribleness

Oh my God, Nan, something truly horrible has happened. Even more horrible than all of the horrible stuff before. After I emailed you yesterday I went to get some bread and milk and stuff from the shops and then, as I was walking back up our road, I heard a rattling engine noise behind me. The rattling engine noise of a taxi. I couldn't bring myself to look round at first. It can't be him, I kept telling myself. He wouldn't risk it. He wouldn't risk going to jail. But then, when the cab still didn't overtake me, my heart started pounding even faster than it did on the night of Bugsy Malone. I tried telling myself it was just a cab for one of the neighbours, and the driver was going slowly because he was trying to find the right house. But then, when I started walking faster, the cab started going faster to keep up. 'It's him, it's him,' the voice in my head screamed. I started to run but I couldn't bring myself to turn around and see who was driving the taxi, I just focused on getting home as fast as I could.

It wasn't until I'd got around the green and within three houses of home that the taxi overtook me, driving up on to the pavement and screeching to a halt on our drive. I jogged to a halt. What was he going to do? What should I do? I stood there on the pavement outside our next door neighbour's house, my hands trembling, and I watched. Slowly the driver's door opened and Tone-Deaf stepped out of the cab. He was wearing his usual outfit of pale-blue jeans and football shirt and had his baseball cap pulled down low over his face. The bright sunshine was beaming down on me like a spotlight, as if it was waiting for me to make a move, but I was frozen with fear. Tone-Deaf slammed the cab door shut behind him and turned to glare at me. I felt something burning at the back of my throat, like I was going to be sick, but I knew I had to do something, I couldn't just stand there, so I started running up the other side of the drive to the front door. 'Mum, Mum!' I yelled. 'He's here. Don't open the door!' But it was too late, the door began to open and I heard his footsteps pounding up the drive behind me. 'I want my daughter,' he yelled, his voice all deep and slurry. Stale beer and cigarette fumes came blasting over my shoulder. 'Angelica!' he yelled. 'Give me my daughter!' I saw Angelica peer out from behind the door, terrified behind her mask of purple and yellow bruises. 'Georgie,' she cried, holding her arm out as if to pull me in, but it was too late. I felt something shove into my back and I went flying to the side, over the rockery and on to the grass.

What happened next is a bit of a blur. I heard my mum scream a piercing scream and when I looked up she was out in the garden holding something and yelling. I squinted against the sunlight. It was Tone-Deaf's golfing umbrella, the one from the pot next to the door. Angelica was waving it at him like a sword. 'Stay away from us,' she yelled. 'Don't you touch my daughters.' If I hadn't been so scared I would have cheered. Tone-Deaf stood there for a moment, his silhouette black and bulky against the sun. I scrambled to my feet and my legs were dotted with wood chippings from the rockery. 'Don't you tell me what to do,' he shouted, taking a step towards her. Somewhere down the street I heard a door slam. Please, someone come and save us, I silently pleaded. Then there was the sound of an upstairs window being opened. We all looked up, shielding our eyes with our hands. It was Michaela. 'Princess,' Tone-Deaf called, his voice instantly softened, 'I've come to take you to your nan's.' Michaela looked down at him and shook her tiny head and said, 'Go away, Daddy.' Tone-Deaf took a step towards the house, but Angelica stepped sideways to block him. 'What's up, Princess? Don't you want to spend some time with your dad?' he shouted. Again Michaela shook her head. I saw Tone-Deaf clench his fists. 'Why not?' Michaela looked away from him, down at the window sill. 'Because you hurt Mummy. I don't want to see you. I'm scared.'

The next bit is all a bit hazy. Tone-Deaf ran to the open front door. Angelica raced towards him and hit him across the back of his thick neck with the umbrella. I saw him turn, about to push her and I went charging at him head first. He spun round and grabbed hold of me, but thankfully at that moment we all heard a high-pitched wail. It was a police siren and then another one, getting louder and louder and closer and closer. Tone-Deaf let go of me and stood rooted to the spot, staring down the road. Angelica opened her hand to me and I saw her pager. 'Bitch!' Tone-Deaf yelled before running off down the drive. But it was too late. Two police cars screeched to a halt at the foot of the drive and within about a second four men in bright yellow jackets and black trousers were swarming on top of him, screaming, 'Get on the floor!' and handcuffing his arms behind his back.

I'm shaking as I type this, Nan, thinking back to what happened. But you were right when you said about the worst times in our lives often being followed by the best. Tone-Deaf is in jail and will stay there till the trial and for the first time in ages I feel free. After the police left yesterday all three of us had a cry, but it was a good kind of cry, if that makes sense. Angelica hugged Michaela and me for ages and said that we were never going to have to be scared again. She was going to see to it that we would all be happy and safe. And although I could feel her trembling I knew she meant every single word. It's weird but it's as if by hitting Tone-Deaf with the umbrella she finally stopped being afraid of him.

When Jamie arrived later he couldn't believe what had happened, but he said that although it must have been terrifying it was definitely for the best. And he was right. It was the most terrifying experience of my entire life, but by Tone-Deaf turning up and breaking his bail conditions it meant he got locked up and now we can all relax for a while. I'm trying not to think about the court case and what will happen then. I know this relief is probably only temporary but at least we now have some time to plan what we're going to do.

I'm in the library at the moment and as soon as I've sent this mail to you I'm going round to Jamie's. He wants us to do some jamming, thinks it will help me take my mind off all that's happened. I don't know what's wrong with me though because I keep feeling as if I could burst into tears. Silly, isn't it? Oh well, thought I'd let you know the latest.

Lots of love,
Georgie xx

Dear Georgie,

You poor, poor darling. How can you say you feel silly for feeling upset? You've just been through a hugely traumatic few days – it's only natural you should feel tearful. I have to admit I was reading your email through my fingers, hardly bearing to scroll down for fear of what was going to happen next. It must have been absolutely horrific for you – thank goodness the police turned up so quickly. It does restore one's faith in the crime prevention service somewhat. Although the monster should never have been allowed bail in the first place.

It sounds as if you could probably all do with a break so I am going to repeat my invitation – please, please, please ask your mum if I can speak with her. I would love it if you all came down here for a few days to have some fun at the seaside and try to forget the horrible events of the past week. Even if you just came down for a day, I'm sure it would help. There is something so therapeutic about putting some physical distance between yourself and your problems – I wonder if that's why Dylan put himself up for that Hollywood role, to get away from all the reminders of his dad. Give your mum my number, Georgie. Or let me have hers and we'll see if we can sort something out. It really troubles me to think that she might have me down as some kind of internet stalker. I really would like the chance to prove to her that I do genuinely care.

Yours in anticipation,
Nan xx

PS: Hope you have fun 'jamming' with Jamie lolwakn (laughing out loud with a knowing nudge!).

....

From: georgie*harris@hotmail.com
To: nancyblue#@aol.com
Date: Fri, 25 August 10:01
Subject: Phone Call

Hi,

Jamming with Jamie was great thanks lolatao (laughing out loud and tingling all over!). He played guitar and I sang a few

286

songs and although it was really lovely I couldn't stop worrying that he would never kiss me again. I was scared that after all the drama of the last few days he wouldn't want to get involved with a family like mine. But then, just as I was having a sip of my Diet Coke, he came over and sat down next to me on the sofa and he took my glass from me and put it on the coffee table and then he kissed me. A proper, slow, French kiss. And although I'd never done one of those before and have always been really stressed at the thought of not knowing what to do with my tongue, it just sort of came naturally and it wasn't gross at all!! (Sorry if this is too much information but I had to share it with someone!) And then he said, all low and gruff, 'Would you like to go out with me?' And I said, 'Where to?' And he said, 'Anywhere, just out with me.' And I still didn't get it so I got up and picked up my jacket and said, 'Yeah, sure.' And he said, 'No, I don't mean go out right now, I mean be my girlfriend.'

I stared at him for a moment and I think my cheeks must have realised what he meant before the rest of me did because they went all hot and then I started to smile and he smiled too, a really lovely sorrowful smile that actually wasn't sorrowful at all and then he got up and gave me a massive hug and said. 'All right, Blousey?' And I said, 'Yeah, Bugsy.' And then we spent the afternoon cuddling and chatting about everything that happened and he asked me loads of questions about my dad, which was lovely because talking about him made it feel as if he was in the room with us. And maybe he was? I hope so. But not during the French kissing part though!!

And I've got some brilliant news! I've just spoken to Angelica and she said it's OK for you to give me a ring on her mobile! I don't know if she'll speak to you though, she's still being a bit weird about us emailing each other, but we can at least try. Her number is 07894 5677789. Give us a ring as soon as you can . . .

Lots of love,
Georgie xxx

....

From: nancyblue#@aol.com
To: georgie*harris@hotmail.com
Date: Fri, 25 August 16:08
Subject: Re: Phone Call

Dearest Georgie,

It was so lovely to speak to you today – so reassuring to hear you sounding so chirpy after all that you've been through. And it was wonderful to finally speak to your mum and reassure her that I'm not insane – well, only in a good way! Do you think she will accept my invitation to come down here? She seemed a little hesitant on the phone, which is completely understandable of course. But at least if she met me she could see that I've only ever had your best interests at heart and then hopefully we could all be friends?

You have to bear with me, Georgie, patience isn't really one of my strongest points. I so badly want to help you all and I get so frustrated stuck here on this computer, able to do diddly squat except send a tumble of words out into cyber space.

Eagerly awaiting your response.

With loads of love as always,
Nan xx

PS: I forgot to congratulate you on your French kiss! Well done, darling, and I'm sure your dad had the decency to look the other way lwwan (laughing whilst winking and nudging!).

....

From: georgie*harris@hotmail.com

To: nancyblue#@aol.com

Date: Sat, 26 August 14:22

Subject: Latest Shock News

Hi Nan,

You are not going to believe the latest news! This morning our phone rang and when Angelica answered it her face literally went as white as a sheet. Even her bruises seemed to go paler purple. 'He's what?' she said, sitting down on one of the kitchen chairs. Tone-Deaf's escaped, was the first thought that entered my mind and I sat down opposite her and searched her face for clues. 'But how? Where? When?' Angelica asked and I could see her bottom lip starting to quiver. I ran over to the back door and shut and bolted it. How could he have escaped? Were we never going to be free of him? Tears began to well in my eyes. It was all so unfair. 'Well, thank you for letting me know,' Angelica said, after listening in silence to the person at the other end for what seemed like forever. Thank you! How could she say thank you to them for letting him loose again? I watched in shock as she attempted to replace the receiver. Her hand was trembling so much the whole phone clunked to the floor. 'What's happened?' I asked, my voice all squeaky. 'Tony,' she whispered, after picking up the phone. 'He's been charged with attempted murder.'

Oh Nan, it was such a weird feeling, sickness and shock and fear and then – and I know this probably sounds really horrible – relief. Do you remember the morning our water was cut off and Tone-Deaf came back from work with his cab window smashed and his hand all cut? Well, apparently he had picked up a Somalian man and when he hadn't got enough money to pay his fare Tone-Deaf got into the back of the cab and beat him almost to death. The police know it was him who did it because they found his DNA on the man where he punched him and the odds of it not being Tone-Deaf are something like one trillion to one. When they arrested him for beating up Angelica, they took a DNA sample and when they entered it into their computer it came up as a match. Apparently the Somalian was left for dead and they don't reckon he'll ever walk again.

After she told me, Angelica went and unbolted and opened the back door. 'It's over,' she said, turning round to face me, tears spilling down her cheeks. 'It's really finally over.' And then we hugged each other for about an hour.

So that's the latest, Nan, I'll be in touch again when the shock has worn off.

Lots of love,
Georgie xx

....

From: nancyblue#@aol.com
To: georgie*harris@hotmail.com
Date: Sat, 26 August 17:05
Subject: Re: Latest Shock News

Oh my goodness – I wish I could say I don't believe it, but unfortunately your latest news rings all too true. It sends shivers down my spine thinking of you living in the same house as that man for so long. Thank goodness he didn't hurt you or your mum any more than he did. At least now you can all be free of him. I was so worried he would manage to twist things and be found not guilty of beating your mum. You hear about that kind of thing happening all the time with domestic violence. At least now he will be in prison for a long, long time and you will all be able to build a new life together away from him. I hope you are all OK. Let me know if you need anything.

All my love,

Nan xxx

....

From: georgie*harris@hotmail.com
To: nancyblue#@aol.com
Date: Sun, 27 August 13:11
Subject: Great news!!

Hi Nan,

Well, the shock is finally starting to wear off. The police reckon Tone-Deaf will be in prison for at least six years. When I first heard that I felt a bit sick. Why can't they lock him up forever? But then I realised that in six years time I'll be twenty! I'll be an adult. And Angelica says six years is plenty of time to build a new life for ourselves. She seems to be getting stronger and happier and more like her old self every day. And guess what? She says we can come down to Brighton for the day! And she said it would be all right to meet up with you.

We just had a really nice chat and she told me that when she first found out we'd been emailing each other she'd been really jealous! Can you imagine that? My mum jealous of me emailing someone! But she told me that she understood why I did it and she said she was really sorry that I felt I couldn't come to her. She told me that she only got drunk to try and blot out the pain of having to live with Tone-Deaf and that from now on she isn't going to touch a drop, to prove to me that she doesn't need to any more. She also said that you sounded really nice on the phone and that she can't wait to meet you!!! And I can't wait to see you again either!

I just looked through some of my earlier mails to you and it's unbelievable how much has changed. At the start of the summer holidays I was so lonely and depressed. I felt like I didn't really belong anywhere – at school, in my family, with my friends. But now I feel as if I fit into my life perfectly. I think I'm going to call this my butterfly summer. Not just because I've had about a thousand butterflies camping in my tummy, but because this was the summer I stopped being a dull old caterpillar, I broke out of my cocoon and I finally found my wings. I've got my old mum back, I've performed a lead part in a show, I stood up to Tone-Deaf, I have a boyfriend, I lost my fake friend and I gained a real friend in you. Thank you so much for everything you've done for me. For listening when no one else would. For making me feel special again.

Earlier this morning, on my way to the high street, I saw Jessica and Kate One walking towards me in the park. At first I felt sick and wished I was with Jamie, but as they got closer something really strange began to happen. I felt this strange unfurling feeling inside me, as if I was growing stronger and freer with every step. When I drew level with them they stopped and Jessica said, in a weird London gangsta accent, 'All right, George. Is it, like, true dat your old man has been banged up for going like, psycho?' I looked at her, my, until recently, so-called best friend, and it felt as if I was looking at a complete stranger. I didn't even feel angry with her for what she'd done. I just felt as if I didn't know her at all. And then, all of a sudden, I really wanted to laugh, because all of a sudden I felt like the grown-up one and she looked like the stupid little kid.

'I tell you what, Jessica,' I said, smiling sweetly, 'why don't you just get a life?' And then I carried on walking, the buttercup-coloured sunlight bouncing off the footpath in front of me, forming my very own yellow brick road.

I'll let you know when Angelica has decided what day we'll be coming down. Cannot wait to see you!

Lots of love,
Georgie xx

From: nancyblue#@aol.com
To: georgie*harris@hotmail.com
Date: Sun, 27 August 16:19
Subject: Re: Great News!!

Hurrah and huzzah! I'm so excited I've just given Woodstock a big sloppy kiss. You know that if you want to invite Jamie down too you'd be more than welcome. The coast can be extremely conducive to romance, all of that fresh air and those crashing waves. And besides, I'm dying to meet him!! Sorry, I'm so nosy it's criminal. I also might have a little surprise for you, darling, but I'm keeping that one firmly under my (witch's) hat.

I'm so pleased your mum is getting better and I cheered out loud when I read about your meeting with the dreaded walking crab stick. 'You go girl!' I yelled at my PC. Poor old Woodstock nearly jumped out of his skin. Ooh, you'll get to meet Woodstock too. You'll love him, darling, and so will your cute little sis. He'll be a real live Tigger for her to play with. He's so full of life I can barely keep up with him.

You really don't have to thank me, you know. If anything I should be the one thanking you. At the start of the summer I was so depressed too. If you were a caterpillar then I was a moth – old and dusty and ready to fling myself into a flame. But you made me want to embrace life again. Despite all of the problems you were going through, your emails were so full of life and hope. I couldn't help but be affected by them. So thank you too, from the bottom of my heart. But enough of this serious talk, it's making me feel as if our friendship is over, and it isn't. It's just another chapter that's coming to a close and now we can both turn the page together. One, two, three . . .

All my love always,
Nan xxx

Part Six

A New Chapter

From: georgie*harris@hotmail.com
To: nancyblue#@aol.com
Date: Thur, 31 August 21:30
Subject: Thank you!!!

Dear Nan,

Thank you so, so much for such a lovely day. We all had a great time. Angelica couldn't stop talking about the super bungee ride all the way home. I still can't believe she went on it — I would have been way too scared I'd fly off the pier and into the sea! It was great to see her being so fearless and fun again though. And Michaela is now obsessed with Woodstock. Good job Jamie took some pictures of him on his phone! They all loved you too by the way, but then I always knew they would. And as for your surprise — well, I don't know what to say, apart from IT WAS FROST-FREE!!!! Good luck with your first day filming. Better go now as have just popped into the internet café on my way back from the station and promised Angelica I wouldn't be long. Can't believe I'm going back to school next Monday!! This summer has flown by — and there was me thinking it was going to be boring!!

Lots of love,
Georgie xxx

From: georgie*harris@hotmail.com

To: dylan+curt@yahoo.com

Date: Thur, 31 August 21:35

Subject: Hello!

Dear Dylan,

It was so nice to meet you at your mum's today and thank you so much for giving me your email address – and promising to answer any of my acting questions. It really means a lot to me as I used to be a big fan of yours when you were in Jessop Close. I'm so glad your film went well and Jamie and I look forward to coming to see you in your play when it opens in London in November. It's so cool that you'll be acting in the very theatre where your parents first met.

Anyway, as I said, it was lovely to meet you and good luck with your rehearsals.

Best wishes,
Georgie x

Acknowledgements

To all of the teenagers who have come to my drama and writing workshops over the years, thank you so much for your energy and enthusiasm. And for inspiring me to write this book. And a massive thank you to everyone who turned *Dear Dylan* from a self-publishing experiment into the stuff that publishing fairy tales are made of. To all of the YA bloggers for their lovely reviews, everyone involved in the Young Minds Book Award who voted for the book, Sara Starbuck, my fellow pirate of the pen, Erzsi Deak, my literary mother hen, Ben Horslen, for showing me how to edit like a true pro, all of my fantastic colleagues at Hothouse Fiction, and last but by no means least, Ali Dougal, Leah Thaxton and the rest of the lovely team at Egmont for making my dream come true.

Turn over for sneak preview of Siobhan Curham's
next stunning novel...

Finding
Cherokee Brown

Prologue

I've decided to write a novel. If I don't write a novel I will kill somebody. And then I will go to jail and knowing my lousy luck end up sharing a cell with a shaven-headed she-he called Jeff who smokes Superkings and thinks it's cool to keep a fifteen-year-old girl as a slave. But if I write a novel I can kill as many people as I like with my words and never have to lick a she-he's boots.

It was Agatha Dashwood who first put the idea of writing a book into my head. Last Saturday afternoon I'd gone down to the Southbank – again – and I was browsing through the tables of second-hand books – again – and there it was, stuffed in between a biography of Princess Diana and *A Complete History of Piston Engines*:

So You Want to Write a Novel? by Agatha Dashwood.

It looked a bit naff to be honest. The photo on the cover was of this fierce old lady glaring over the rim of her glasses like some kind of psycho librarian. But the first thing I thought when I read the title was, yes – *I do*. Which was a bit weird because I'd never thought of writing a novel before. So I picked the book up and did my usual page 123 test. I do this whenever I'm deciding whether to buy a book. I don't bother reading the blurb on the back, or the first page – the writer's obviously going to be trying their hardest there, aren't they?

It's how they're getting on by page 123 that's the real test. If they're crap at writing or bored with their story then you can bet they won't be making any effort at all by that point. So I flicked through the yellowing pages, trying not to gag on the musty smell filling the air, and this is what it said at the top of page 123:

The Authentic Novelist Writes about What They Know

Aspiring novelist, if you want your writing to ring true; for your words to echo around your reader's head with passion and clarity, like church bells calling worshippers to mass, then you have to write about what you know.

I know the church bells and worshippers stuff is a bit naff, but the rest of it made the hairs on the back of my neck prickle. I snapped the book shut and took it over to pay. With Agatha Dashwood's help I was going to write a novel about my crappy life but, unlike my crappy life, it wouldn't be dictated by my mum or Alan or the brain-deads at school or any of my stupid teachers. It would be my story. Told my way.

NOTEBOOK EXTRACT
Character Questionnaire No. 1

When I started out in my writing career, many years ago, writing short stories and serials for The Respected Lady magazine, the Character Questionnaire became my most cherished friend. Use the template below before you start your story to get to know your own characters even better than you know yourself.

Agatha Dashwood, *So You Want to Write a Novel*

Okay, I've got a bit of a problem. I've been trying to do a Character Questionnaire on my main character – namely me. And that's the problem: the 'namely' bit. I mean, who would choose to call their main character Claire Weeks? It's hardly exciting is it? Hardly the name of a kick-ass heroine. Well, I'll just have to invent myself a new name. A heroic name. A name that will sit proudly alongside Anne Frank and Laura Ingalls Wilder on bookshelves and not want to cower in embarrassment.

Possible Kick-Ass Literary Names:

Roxy Montana – too much like Hannah?

Ruby Fire – naff!

Laura Wild – too similar to one of my own literary heroines.

Anna Franklyn – ditto.

Jet Steele – sounds like a female wrestler.

Okay, I'll come back to my name later or I'll never get started on the book. I'll stay as Claire for now. And keep my surname as Weeks, even though it sounds like 'weak'. Just another great thing to thank my step-dad Alan for I guess. Along with a knowledge of Neil Diamond that borders on child abuse.

In case you have the kind of parents who actually listen to music from after 1980, Neil Diamond is this dorky American guy who sings about girls called 'Cracklin' Rosie' and 'Sweet Caroline'. Seriously lame. Just like Alan. And you should see the shirts he wears; bright blue shiny satin WITH SEQUINS. Neil Diamond I mean, not Alan. Alan just wears boring suits with lairy, look-at-me-I'm-oh-so-wacky ties or, even worse, on what he calls 'dress-down-days' he wears denim shirts TUCKED IN to his jeans. WITH SHINY LEATHER LACE-UP SHOES. Is it any wonder I've been driven to seek refuge in the world of literature?

Anyway, back to the Questionnaire:

Character's Name: Claire Weeks (soon to be changed to something way better).

Character's Age: 15 (well, 15 in one day's time).

Briefly describe your character's appearance: She is short and thin, with dark brown shoulder-length hair and brown eyes. She needs a radical makeover.

What kind of clothes do they wear? Black.

How do they get on with their parents? They don't.

What physical objects do they associate with their parents? An i-phone permanently attached to her step-dad's hand like some kind of growth. And a collection of tracksuits in every colour of the rainbow for her mum.

Do they have any brothers or sisters? No, but they have a couple of alien life-forms from the Planet Obnoxious posing as seven-year-old twin brothers.

Think of one positive and one negative event from their past and how it has shaped them? Only one negative? Okay, this might take a while to narrow down. The first thing that springs to mind is the day Helen moved away to Bognor Regis. This was mortally negative on two counts: firstly, I lost my one true friend and secondly, who wants to live in a place that is named after a bog? Seriously! And just because some bright spark added the word Regis (which I think means royal) it doesn't make it any less bog-sounding. Then there was the time last summer when I wanted to go to the Hyde Park Music Festival, but Alan said I couldn't because Jay-Z was headlining and he felt that listening to too much rap music would be 'bad for my personal development'. Like listening to Neil Diamond droning on about being 'forever in blue jeans' isn't?!! Of course, my mum agreed with him. She always agrees with Alan because he is a life coach and therefore 'an expert at life'. I'm not so sure about that. As far as I can tell, being a life coach basically means that you charge people a load of money to tell them how messed up their lives are and then charge them another load to tell them they need to fix it.

Alan's company is called 'OH YES YOU CAN!' and he likes to do those really annoying mimed speech mark things with his fingers whenever he's talking and wants to emphasise a word. For example, when I told him that I don't even like rap and I actually wanted to go to the music festival to see the rock band Screaming Death he looked at me and sighed and said, 'I don't really think that subjecting yourself to a day of heavy metal would really be "*helpful*" for your personal development either, Claire.' And he wiggled two fingers on each hand around the word helpful. Personally I think he is a "complete moron".

Right, better try and think of a positive event for my character. There was the moment I made friends with Helen, on our first day at Rayners High. I'd been sitting in our classroom, faking smiles like I had a twitch while all the time thinking, Oh God, why couldn't I have been born in 1867 to a pioneer family in the American Midwest and only have to worry about making it through the next winter rather than seven long years at high school. But then, when one of the boys started teasing this Asian girl and everyone else started laughing like a load of baaing sheep, I caught sight of Helen. I could see from the way she was frowning that she was thinking the exact same as me – this boy is a total loser. As soon as I managed to make eye-contact with her I sort of raised one eyebrow, the way I'd seen this sarcastic cop character do on TV, and she did the same back and then we both started smiling – but proper, mean-it smiles rather than oh-my-god-my-jaw-is-going-to-break-if-I-have-to-prop-this-thing-up-any-longer kind of smiles.

That was a whole four years ago now. It's been six months since Helen moved away. Her leaving is another reason for me writing a book. I don't really have anyone to talk to anymore – not anyone who gets me. And the great thing about having an imaginary reader is that you can write exactly what you want, how you want, and you can at least pretend that they'll like and understand you. And won't want to beat you up or call you names.

How does your character speak? Too fast apparently, at least according to her mum and Miss Davis, her chronically deaf form-tutor.

What is their favourite meal? Fish and chips wrapped in paper, with loads of salt and vinegar, outside on a freezing cold day.

Do they believe in God? No. Don't know. Maybe. But not a God with a long white beard who sits on a cloud. I gave up on that one the year we went to Florida and I stared out of the window looking for God for the entire eight-hour flight. No-one lives on clouds. At all.

What is their bedroom like? Full of books. And full of mess according to my mum, but she doesn't get it. I know where everything is and I like having everything close to hand, not shut away in cupboards or filed away on shelves like everything else in our house.

What is your character's motto in life? Tidying is for wimps. And cleaning is for people with way too much time on their hands who should be made to move somewhere deadly dull – like Bognor Regis.

Does your character have any secrets? Yes. Since Helen left she has skipped school three times to go up to the Southbank to people-watch for the day. And although everyone in her class – including her teacher – knows that she is being bullied, her parents don't. What a great secret!

What makes them jealous? People who are happy and don't ever get picked on.

Do they have any pets? No, because a stray dog hair or morsel of cat food might get on to the carpet and cause their parents to have a total freak-out.

Is their glass half full? She's currently drinking a can – of Dr Pepper – and it's nearly empty. Bit of a random question!

Have they ever lost anyone dear to them? Helen when she moved away. And I guess there's my real dad. Although he left when I was just a baby and moved to America 'because he had commitment issues and was incapable of growing up' according to my mum, and I've never seen him since. Can you lose something if you can't remember ever having it?

Who do they most admire? Laura Ingalls Wilder and Anne Frank.

Are they popular? No. But she doesn't care because she wouldn't want to be popular with a load of morons and wannabe gangsters anyway.

Do they love themselves? No, of course not!

What is their motivating force in life? To get through a day without being beaten up.

What is their core need in life? To not feel like the wrong part in a jigsaw all of the time.

What is their mindset at the beginning of your story and what do they want? She is mortally fed-up and she wants to change everything. Everything.

Meet ~~SIOBHAN CURHAM~~

Hi, Siobhan! Your lovely readers would like to get to know you. Can you tell us a bit about your childhood?

I grew up on a council estate in North London. Our house had a lot of kids (I'm the eldest of four) and a LOT of books. Both of my parents are total book worms and I definitely inherited their love of reading. The happiest times of my childhood were when I had my nose in a book — and my mouth full of cake!

What about your teenage years. Did you have any celeb crushes like Georgie's?

I don't think there was a single second of my teenage years when I didn't have a crush on one celeb or another. The only one I ever wrote to was the singer from a band called The Thompson Twins. I was overjoyed when he sent me back a postcard from Arizona, where they were on tour.

In *Dear Dylan*, Georgie discovers that she's a talented singer. Other than writing, do you have any special talents?

I played the flute to Grade 8 and even got to play at the Royal Albert Hall, but I gave it up when I was 15 because I didn't think it was 'rock'n'roll' enough!

And is there anything you *wish* you could do, but can't?

I wish I could sing so well I could move people to tears. Unfortunately, when I do start singing, I only seem to move people to leave.

Describe yourself in five words.

Dreamer, writer, joker, optimist, cake-oholic.

What inspired you to write this particular story, and how did you come up with the character of Georgie? Why did you decide to use emails?

The original idea came from an article I read about a woman who started writing fan mail to the Beatle George Harrison when she was a teenager back in the sixties. Because George was so busy being a mega famous popstar his mum was handling his written correspondence. The girl and his mum ended up becoming penpals for years and I loved the idea of a young girl and a much older woman striking up a friendship purely through letters. I used emails in *Dear Dylan* because this is how most people communicate these days. The character of Georgie was inspired in part by a girl who came to one of my drama workshops. She lived in foster care and had been through a lot in her life and yet she was still so full of spirit and fun. She made me want to write about a character who never gave up on her dream, no matter what problems life threw at her.

Who are your favourite fictional characters? And do you have any personal heroes?

My favourite characters are Holden Caulfield from *The Catcher in the Rye* and Lennie from *The Sky is Everywhere*. One of my biggest heroes is the author Judy Blume. I love the way she writes about emotional issues in such a tender, entertaining and thoughtful way. I found reading her books very reassuring when I was going through difficult times as a young teenager.

Have you had any embarrassing moments, like the day Georgie puts oil in her hair and can't wash it out?

Oh, yes! The most recent one was when I tucked the back of my skirt into my tights at work. I didn't realize why people were sniggering until I had done the walk of shame all the way through the building back to my desk!

What's your motto in life?

Dare to dream.

Pick five songs that would be on the *Dear Dylan* soundtrack.

Well, *Wonderful Tonight* by Eric Clapton and *Ordinary Fool* from Bugsy Malone actually feature in the book. Other songs that sum up the theme of the book are *Lose Yourself* by Enimem, *If I Can Dream* by Elvis and *Somewhere Over the Rainbow*.

**Can you tell us anything about your next book,
Finding Cherokee Brown? (There's a sneaky peak in
here too!)**

I wrote *Finding Cherokee Brown* in response to a letter a teenage
girl had written in to a magazine I was working for. She was
complaining about the lack of feisty female characters in YA
fiction and how she was tired of reading about girls who
couldn't function unless they met Mister Right. I cut the
letter out, pinned it to my noticeboard and used it as a
challenge. The girl's name was Cherokee. I really hope I've
created a namesake she would want to read about!

Do you have any advice for aspiring writers?

Yes, like Georgie in *Dear Dylan*, never give up on your dream.
And write about things you feel passionately about. That
passion will shine out from the page.

**And finally – tell us one thing about yourself that
not many people know . . .**

I have a Russian middle name – Raissa!

ELECTRIC MONKEY

To find out more about Siobhan Curham and other books for young adult readers check out the brilliant new **ELECTRIC MONKEY** website:

Trailers

Siobhan's blog

News and Reviews

Competitions

Downloads

Free stuff

Author interviews

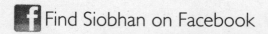Find Siobhan on Facebook

www.electricmonkeybooks.co.uk